"Don't shoot!"

Angela added under her breath, "Please, please don't shoot." Closing her eyes, she stepped out from behind the relative safety of the car with her hands held high.

This was by far her dumbest decision to date. And the longer she stood in the middle of the road, the longer she proved that.

"You can put your hands down."

Angela whirled around.

A one-eyed grizzly bear of a man wore mud-colored camouflage and cradled a military-grade rifle with a high-powered scope in his hands As big as he was, he'd somehow snuck up along the passenger side of the car.

Angela drew courage from the fact that he wasn't pointing his weapon at her. "You should put that away before someone gets hurt. Namely me."

"Missed you by a mile." He propped himself against the vehicle and drilled her with his single-eyed stare. "Then again, my aim isn't what it used to be."

Dear Reader,

According to Department of Defense statistics from 2008, there are 73,000 single parents serving in the United States military. Those widowed, divorced or who have given birth after enlistment account for some 5.3% of the overall military.

Single applicants with custody of a child under the age of eighteen are ineligible for enlistment. There are single parents who fight their way around these regulations by giving up custody or marrying for convenience in order to join the military.

This story falls into that gray area.

From the moment single mom Angela Adams walked into the recruiting office in *Mitzi's Marine* and marine recruiter gunnery sergeant Bruce Calhoun sent her to Wyoming, I knew I had to write her story.

She was young. And pretty. And desperate.

"I might know a guy." He scribbled directions on the back of his business card. "Lives in Wyoming. Doesn't have a phone. He's angry at the world right now. But he might marry you on paper. If just to get back at Uncle Sam." He handed her the card. "What's your name?"

"Angela," she said.

I hope you enjoy Angela and Hatch's story.

Rogenna Brewer

Marry Me, Marine
Rogenna Brewer

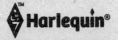

TORONTO NEW YORK LONDON
AMSTERDAM PARIS SYDNEY HAMBURG
STOCKHOLM ATHENS TOKYO MILAN MADRID
PRAGUE WARSAW BUDAPEST AUCKLAND

Recycling programs
for this product may
not exist in your area.

ISBN-13: 978-0-373-71759-0

MARRY ME, MARINE

www.Harlequin.com

Printed in U.S.A.

ABOUT THE AUTHOR

When an aptitude test labeled her suited for being a librarian or working in the clergy, Rogenna tried to shake that good girl image by joining the United States Navy. Ever the rebel, she landed in the chaplain's office, where duties included operating the base library. The irony of that did not escape her. A romantic adventurer at heart, Rogenna served navy, coast guard and marine corps personnel as a chaplain's yeoman in such exotic locales as Midway Island and the Pentagon. She is an excellent marksman with an unusual handicap that came in handy when writing this story. She shoots right-handed, sighting with her left eye because of poor eyesight in her right eye. A habit she has yet to change even though she's seeing the world in a whole new light after corrective surgery.

Books by Rogenna Brewer

HARLEQUIN SUPERROMANCE

Other titles by this author available in ebook format

This one is for my editor, Victoria Curran.
It's an honor and a privilege working with you.

And to the 73,000 single parents serving in the
United States military.

Special thanks to Shanna for letting me use her
twins' candy heart story.

To Omni Eye Specialists, Spivack Vision Center
and Madison Street Surgery Center, especially
Dr. Amiel and his surgical staff for taking such
good care of me.

And to my eye doctor, Dr. Gosling of Optical
Matters. I haven't taken out any more right side
mirrors while backing out of the garage.

CHAPTER ONE

EXCEPT FOR THAT TRIP to Yellowstone with her parents the summer she turned nine, Angela Adams had never ventured north of the Colorado state line into Wyoming. Had never taken I-80 west into unfamiliar territory. Certainly not to propose marriage to a man she'd never met.

Fumbling with the map, hastily scribbled on a napkin, she tried to decipher her own handwriting. "Water pump mailbox?"

The answer appeared on her left, a weathered mailbox mounted on an old wrought-iron pump. The missing letters made the name impossible to read. Ignoring the clamor in her head telling her to keep driving straight through the Cowboy State, she slowed to take the unmarked dirt road.

Life so far had been a series of bad choices. Whether she was on the right track now or taking another wrong turn was hard to know. Several bumpy miles later the tires of Grandma Shirley's pink 1980 Cadillac Seville rumbled over a cattle guard, jolting Angela back to reality.

With enough steam rising from beneath the hood to rival Old Faithful, Angela pulled to the side of the road before the engine could vapor-lock on her again. Her grandmother may have been a top-selling Mary Kay rep to win this car, but that was more than thirty years ago.

Long before Angela was born.

The sloped trunk gave the Caddy the look of a classic Rolls Royce, but there was vintage and then there was old. With a sigh of resignation Angela shut down the engine.

She'd seriously underestimated the amount of coolant needed to get her this far. Resisting the urge to drop her head to the steering wheel, she popped the catch for the hood and stepped into the crisp air of a mid-November afternoon.

Once she'd rounded the car she raised the hood—and choked on the smell of burned crayon. With the red rag from her jeans pocket she tested the too-hot-to-handle radiator cap and—

The first ping got her attention. The second, definitely a gunshot, had her ducking for cover behind the Caddy's shiny grill.

Heart pounding, Angela glanced over her shoulder at the bullet-ridden no trespassing sign swinging from a rusted-off-its-hinges cattle gate, half-hidden in the scrub. Granted, the sign was several yards to her right, but she'd never been downrange of gunfire before.

Her recruiter wouldn't have sent her here were she in any real danger. Would he? He'd merely said, "I might know a guy."

On the off chance that this "guy" with no cell phone and no computer would say yes to her proposal, she'd driven four hundred miles with a leaky radiator and next to no gas money in her pocket. She'd need more than a couple well-intentioned warning shots to scare her off.

She'd left Denver with little more than the guy's name and whereabouts written on the back of her recruiter's business card. But in the town of Henry's Fork, where she'd stopped for further directions, folks had warned her he'd likely shoot first and ask questions later.

Angela raised the dirty red rag. She didn't have a white one to signal surrender.

When he didn't shoot the rag out of her hand she took it as a good sign. In case it wasn't, she got out her cell phone and searched for a signal so she could call for help. She didn't know how long she crouched by the car—but several hundred heartbeats passed. Was she supposed to just wait him out?

She glanced at her smartphone. Not so smart. Still no signal.

Closing her eyes, she took a deep enough breath to give herself the courage to stand, and moved from the relative safety of the Cadillac, her hands held high. "I'm coming out! Please, please don't shoot."

Surrounded by barren trees, she scanned the bluffs. No sign of life anywhere. Even the dry creek bed appeared dead. A lone brown leaf blew from one rock to the next. Dressed in her Ugg boots and matching suede and lamb's wool vest, Angela stood in the middle of the dirt road, unsure of her next move.

This was by far her dumbest idea to date. And the longer she stood there, rag and phone in the air, the more she proved that.

What was he waiting for? Was he watching her now?

The wind kicked up and she shivered.

"You can put your hands down, darlin'"

Angela whirled.

The one-eyed grizzly bear of a man wore mud-colored camouflage and cradled a military-grade rifle with a high-powered scope in hands sporting fingerless rawhide gloves. As big as he was, he'd somehow sneaked up along the passenger side of the car.

Well, at least he wasn't pointing his weapon at her. "You should put that away before someone gets hurt," she said.

"Missed you by a mile." He propped himself against Shirley's prized possession and drilled Angela with his single-eyed stare. "Then again, my aim ain't what it used to be."

She shifted her gaze from his piercing-blue left eye to the black patch over his right. With his overlong hair hanging in his face and his overgrown beard shading the rest of it, she couldn't read his expression. But he had to be kidding, right?

Civilized people didn't go around shooting each other.

Oh, wait—yes, they did. And he fit the stereotype. Ex-military. Loner. "But he was always so quiet," the neighbors would say when the media interviewed them. What had the townspeople called him? The Hermit of Henry's Fork?

The guffaws of the old men sitting at the counter in the diner, drinking their coffee black and eating their pie à la mode, mocked her now. "We tried to tell her."

She glanced at the sign. "You dotted the *i* in no trespassing from what, a good two hundred yards out?" She had no idea what she was talking about. Except her dad had taken her to a rifle range once.

"Nice to know you can read. The private property signs start a mile back. Once your car cools down I expect you to turn around and get yourself headed the right way."

So much for small talk.

Angela twisted the rag in her hands. "I'm not lost."

"What are you, then?" He eyed her curiously.

"Looking for you."

"I'm not a novelty act, darlin'. You need to get the hell off my property." He pushed away from the Caddy and continued in the direction Angela had been driving. As he passed the sign, he tapped it with the butt end of his rifle. "I wasn't aiming to dot the *i*. Next time I won't miss."

Under different circumstances she might have let him scare her off. His calmness seemed even more dangerous than his weapon. But she'd come to know the worst kind of fear: desperation. And she'd driven too far to give up now. "Please, Hatch!"

He ground to a halt. "Do we know each other?"

Even if he hadn't emphasized the word *know,*

Angela would have felt his meaning in the way he looked at her. As if every inch of her was his for the taking. Heat crept into her cheeks as she shook her head.

"Who sent you?" His question and the way he scanned their surroundings showed an edge of paranoia.

He moved in so close she had to scrunch her nose. He smelled...earthy. And that was being kind.

Was this really the man she wanted to marry?

Building hysteria bubbled at the back of her throat. Did what she want matter anymore? A short laugh escaped. "Nobody."

He cocked an eyebrow. "Liar."

Startled by the clarity of his gaze, she found herself searching his face. If eyes were the windows to the soul, then his was dark and stormy. But not out of touch with reality.

His pupil appeared normal. Black like onyx and in sharp contrast to the cobalt-blue iris, somehow softened by spiky black lashes.

"Don't make me ask you again."

An unexpected jolt of electricity shot through her at the intensity of his stare. "My recruiter thought maybe you'd help me."

"Your recruiter?"

"Bruce Calhoun."

"Ah." He took a step back and studied her with renewed interest. "Help you how?"

"I need a husband."

"And I'm supposed to find one for you?"

The rag in her hand became a tangled knot. "You're the one." Her words sounded more like a question than a statement.

He let out a snort, but at least he'd found some humor in her announcement. "Tell my buddy Bruce Calhoun that's the best laugh I've had in a long time. Thanks, but no thanks. I don't need a wife."

"It's not like I want an actual husband." She recoiled at the thought. "Just a piece of paper that says I have one. To enlist."

So much for appealing to, what, his sense of duty?

Patriotism? Pride?

Loyalty to the gunnery sergeant who'd sent her here? Why would the man standing here, or any man for that matter, marry her so she could join the Marine Corps? He'd have to be loony.

And while this might be debatable she hoped he wasn't *that* crazy. Just crazy enough to say yes.

He continued to scrutinize her. "The only

reason you'd need a husband to enlist would be that you're a single mom."

Was that common knowledge to everyone except her? She hadn't realized it, walking into the recruiting office with her high ideal of providing a better life for her son.

Just thinking of Ryder bolstered her determination.

"He's two. Almost two and a half. His birthday is in May." She flashed a cell phone picture of her son in his Halloween costume. Dressed like Yoda from *Star Wars*. He had her red hair and green eyes. "His name is Ryder."

Seeing the man's lack of interest in her digitized family album, she tucked her phone away with a sinking feeling. If pictures of Ryder didn't tug at his heartstrings, he had no strings to tug.

"How old are you?" His focus narrowed. He was about to judge her the way most people did— too young and too irresponsible to be a good parent. Well, she *was* a good parent.

"None of your business."

"You just made it my business."

Crossing her arms, she tilted her chin. "Twenty."

He cursed under his breath. "How old do you think I am?"

Hard to say. Beneath all that hair he could be

in his late twenties or early forties, or any age in between. "Old enough," she ventured.

"I need a kid even less than I need a wife."

Angela got the distinct impression he wasn't talking about her son. The man pivoted and started walking away again. She tossed the knotted rag in the general direction of the car and ran to keep up.

"You'll never have to see me again, I promise. Except for the divorce. And that could be anytime after boot camp. Say a year from now—"

"Not going to happen."

She really needed for this to happen. "Hatch, please. Please." How pathetic was she, begging the man to marry her? But right now, saving her pride was secondary to gaining his help. While the military didn't allow single parents to enlist, they did allow parents to serve if they became single *after* enlisting. "I'm not asking for a lifetime commitment."

All she wanted was a piece of paper.

"What part of no don't you understand?"

Even with her long legs she had a hard time keeping up with him in his determination to get away from her. "You haven't said no yet."

He stopped so abruptly she stumbled into him, a solid wall of stubbornness. The look he con-

veyed over his shoulder told her she was pressing
more than just his firm backside.

"I was aiming for the *O* in No. Do I have to
spell it out? Consider that my answer for everything."

"Oh." But that shouldn't count. He'd shot at the
sign before he knew her question.

They'd reached the end of a tree-lined drive.
Before her sat a two-story farmhouse. White or
gray—she couldn't be sure, glancing at the peeling paint. Darker gray shutters hung crookedly
beside cracked and broken windows.

Did anyone actually live here?

Out buildings, including stables and a barn,
divided the sizable clearing into a working ranch
compound. But "run to the ground" didn't begin
to describe it. It was as desolate as the late-
autumn landscape. "How big is your ranch?"

"Six hundred and fifty acres. What's left of it,
anyway."

That sounded big. It looked big enough to her.
But something was missing. "Where is everybody?"

"I'm it." He headed toward an extended-cab
Ford F-150 parked beneath an ancient cottonwood
tree. The shiny black pickup appeared out of place
in the empty yard.

"What about cows?"

"Cattle," he corrected. "What about 'em?"

"Where are they? And horses?"

"All gone. Any more questions?" he asked, lowering the Ford's tailgate and setting his rifle inside.

"Just one." Angela nodded toward the skinned carcass, headless and hanging upside down from the tree, hidden from earlier view by the truck. "What's that?"

"Know anything about field dressing a deer?"

"No," she admitted.

"Too bad." He unfolded a leather pouch, uncovering a hacksaw and a row of very sharp, very lethal looking knives. "Had my heart set on a gal who could field dress a fresh kill."

The knives, the discarded hooves, the bucket of bloody entrails, the stained rubber gloves—they weren't making her queasy. Or even the severed head of a buck staring at her from the truck bed with glassy eyes.

Really, they weren't.

She'd known going into this that she had only one thing a man might want in exchange for a marriage certificate. And just the thought made her want to hurl all over his work boots.

HATCH CAUGHT HER before she hit the ground.

After laying her out across the tailgate, he used his jacket to pillow her head, shaking his. City girl.

Girl being the operative word here. She was little more than a kid out of high school.

Seeing the world though a high-powered scope tended to put things in perspective. He'd felt her apprehension even at a distance. Had assumed a couple warning shots would scare her off. But she was either a whole lot dumber or a whole lot more determined than he'd first given her credit for.

Leaning into the truck bed, he pulled the tarp over his other doe-eyed trophy and waited for the living, breathing one to come around. Long lashes fluttered against the kind of dark smudges that resulted from too many sleepless nights.

She opened her green eyes wide. "Am I still in one piece?"

"What do you think?"

"I'm trying not to think." She glanced toward the tarp-covered buck and sat up.

"Hold on." He tossed off his shooting glove and rolled up his shirtsleeve to fish the icy waters of his beer cooler for a can of cola. He switched hands and passed it to her, shaking the feeling back into his cold, wet one.

"Thank you." Her bangs fell forward onto one flushed cheek and she tucked them behind her ear. At least her color was returning.

Peaches and cream.

An honest to goodness redhead, not the drugstore kind.

Even without the ponytail and smattering of freckles she'd look like jailbait. She wasn't old enough to have a drink with him, yet she'd driven the interstate to marry him.

As a teen mom she'd had all the responsibilities and none of the privileges of adulthood. Twenty still wasn't old enough to know what she wanted in life, let alone marriage.

The Marine Corps? Marriage without commitment?

To a guy she didn't even know? And wouldn't care to know under normal circumstances.

What the hell was she thinking?

What the hell was Calhoun thinking? For the life of him, Hatch couldn't figure out why the gunnery sergeant would send her here. He and Calhoun had bled together on a joint Navy-Marine task force. That made them brothers of sorts.

But brothers had your back.

They didn't send a barely legal young woman

to rattle your cage when all you wanted was to be left alone.

"Since we've established I don't maim for sport and you faint at the drop of a hat—" he nodded toward the carcass "—guess I'd better bag this bad boy." He rolled up his other sleeve and slipped a breathable sack over the meat. "You might want to set your sights on a career path other than the Marine Corps."

After tying off the sack, he raised the hoist.

The meat needed a good six hours to cool. It could wait. She couldn't. Someone had to give this chick a reality check. "Maybe the Navy's more your style, a nice cushy job aboard an aircraft carrier. Like explosive ordnance handler?"

Those bombs could weigh her down so a strong wind wouldn't blow her overboard. Despite her height, which he put around five foot ten, she was a featherweight.

Still, she'd have to have a husband just to join.

"I tried there first," she said in all seriousness. "They didn't want me." She looked down at the can of ginger ale in her hands. "The Marine recruiter..." She shrugged. "He suggested I come see you."

She lifted hopeful eyes to Hatch. If he was her only hope, she was shit out of luck. He didn't want any more needy women in his life. He'd returned home to put all that behind him.

"What about the boy's father?"

"What about him?"

"He'd be the logical choice for a husband. There's a reason the armed services don't allow single parents to enlist." Resisting the urge to remove his patch and show her just how ugly war could get, Hatch continued to try to make some sense of her request. "Selling cosmetics doesn't seem like such a bad way to make a living."

He didn't know jack about that biz, but he did know cars. So unless she'd carjacked an elderly Mary Kay lady for that pink prize, he couldn't figure out how she'd gotten it. That specialty Seville was at least as old as he was, and wasn't the kind of vehicle offered up for sale, even used.

But that didn't mean she couldn't earn one of her own. How hard could it be for a woman to sell lipstick to other women? Although Peaches looked more all-natural pretty than put-together pretty. He'd bet she hadn't even reached her full beauty potential. Given a few more years and the confidence to carry it off, she'd be a real knockout.

"I'm not much of a salesperson." She dismissed

the idea as if she'd heard it before. Pride kept her chin up and her eyes focused on him.

Eyes like that could get a man in trouble. Not jewel-toned. That would have overpowered her pretty complexion. But earth-toned. Soft like a bed of moss in springtime.

Which would have been a decent analogy if his thoughts hadn't strayed to laying her down in it. He liked his women lean and leggy.

He shook his head to clear it.

What the hell was he thinking?

She was too young and too damn wholesome for him. Plenty of guys her own age would jump at the chance to marry her.

So why him? She didn't know him. Or she'd realize he wasn't even a good temporary solution for her particular situation. At the very least she should have taken one look at him and run.

But she hadn't. She was sitting there eyeing him as though he had the answer to all life's problems. Like she was his kid sister, for crying out loud. Hell, Jessie, his own sister, would have been about her age had she lived to see twenty.

He scrubbed a hand over his beard and folded his arms.

"What about family? Your parents couldn't approve of this trip." Although her coming here in the first place suggested a lack of parental guidance.

"There's only my grandma Shirley and me. And Ryder." His trespasser set those soft, mossy-green eyes on him. "I'm prepared to make whatever sacrifices I have to in order to join the military. Being a single mom isn't any easier as a civilian."

He didn't doubt that.

"I think," he said, choosing his next words carefully, "you've been misinformed." He leveled his gaze on her. "If you want me to track down the boy's father, I can do that. I'll even waive my usual fee and throw in a shotgun wedding."

She blinked, clearly puzzled.

Apparently shotgun humor went way over her head.

"Are you some sort of goon for hire?"

"Beats groom for hire. Either way, you couldn't afford me."

Those odd jobs on the fringe of his former career as a Navy SEAL had gotten him through this past year. But jobs for a peripherally challenged operative were few and far between. In fact, her broken-down Cadillac was the most excitement he'd had in a long time.

He reached into the truck bed toolbox and

grabbed a gallon jug of coolant. "Now if you'll excuse me—" he nodded toward her car "—I have goon business to attend to."

His mistake was in turning his back on her.

Halfway down the road he heard the screen door slam. The hollow sound echoed through his memory. All those times he'd tried to leave and couldn't, because his mother had begged him to stay, even as she'd crowded him out with all her crap.

The last time, he'd let the door slam.

At age seventeen.

The military had seemed like his only way out. But he'd needed a parent's signature to join.

His mother had refused, as he knew she would. But he could always count on his father to be drunk enough not to know or care what he was signing. So Hatch had driven to Laramie, found the old man in one of his shit-hole bars and said his goodbyes.

He'd never blamed his father for leaving.

Only for leaving him behind.

Which was what had drawn him to the Teams. The military wasn't just a job. It was a lifestyle. He understood the appeal of that for himself. He couldn't see it for her.

After turning around he set the coolant jug on

the tailgate, he took a deep breath and followed her inside. She'd stopped three feet from the kitchen, and was holding the crook of her arm up to her nose. The stench was enough to put anyone off, but she couldn't have gone any farther had she wanted to.

Worse than the floor-to-ceiling trash were the treasures that reminded him he'd once called this place home—the refrigerator magnet holding his sixth-grade photo; the teapot with the broken handle, still on the windowsill and littered with dried leaves.

The house had always been what family and friends referred to as a tidy mess. Meaning that at one time his mother had at least attempted to control her compulsion, even though the house had always gotten the better of her.

His parents had fought over the messiness in their lives. The lack of money. Love. Kindness and respect.

He'd been too young to make the connection. His mother's need to fill the void with stuff was part of a vicious cycle. Her collecting got worse after his baby sister died, and again after his dad left. Hatch had always known his mother's hoarding would get the best of her. The only thing he'd

CHAPTER TWO

"I'M SORRY." ANGELA apologized again from the passenger seat of his pickup. The man beside her gripped the steering wheel as if maintaining control of his anger depended on it.

What did he have to be angry about?

They were on their way into town—to the auto parts store—for a tire she hadn't known she needed and a water pump she knew she couldn't afford. He turned right onto the highway at the mailbox.

Had to be some irony in there somewhere.

Angela stared out the window, wondering if her grandmother would be able to wire enough money to cover the cost of repairs. And just how was Angela supposed to explain being in Wyoming? Not to mention her reason for being here.

He'd hauled her out of the house and into the cab of his pickup so fast her head was still spinning. She was surprised he hadn't dumped her by the side of the road. Instead, he'd cursed the lug taken with him when he left was the guilt of knowing that.

And leaving, anyway.

Because things got even worse after that.

Peaches lowered her arm and offered a weak smile. "Uh, who died in here?"

"My mother."

nuts and her lack of a spare, took one look under the hood and ordered her back in his truck.

How could a man with one eye even have a driver's license?

She met his hard stare in the extra-wide sideview mirror and sank farther into the bucket seat. "I was just looking for a bathroom."

"They haven't been usable in years."

"Then where—"

"Not there." He'd cut her off, but hadn't answered her question. So where was she supposed to go? And where did *he* go?

And where did he live if "not there"?

She found it hard to imagine anyone living in that house with or without plumbing. But someone had lived there and died there. He didn't elaborate, and several miles passed before Angela got the nerve to ask about his mother. "How long ago did she die?"

"There are no dead bodies in the house, if that's what you're getting at."

It wasn't.

But if he wasn't going to accept her attempt to make peace, then why should she tiptoe around? "Good to know you're not a cross-dressing psychopath."

Other than muttering something about a cold

day in hell, he let the Norman Bates *Psycho* reference slide.

A trace of wood smoke lingered in the cab, together with the pine-scented air freshener. Or was that Irish Spring? He'd shed the outer layer of dirt along with his outerwear.

Shedding her perceptions would take a lot longer.

He glanced at her in the side-view mirror again. "You know the opening scene of every teen horror movie—young woman, healthy lungs, goes looking for trouble and finds it? You're that girl."

Angela rolled her eyes. "You're not as scary as you think you are."

"And you're not as tough."

"I'm a lot tougher than you know." She went back to staring out the window. A *lot* tougher.

The abruptness with which he returned his attention to the road signaled an end to their conversation. They continued in silence for several more miles, and she took full advantage of his blind side.

What did he look like under all that scraggly hair? With a little imagination, kinda like a roughed-up version of Alex O'Loughlin.

First impressions weren't always right.

A jean jacket had replaced the heavy down coat

and coveralls. Underneath that camouflage outerwear, he'd had on a clean chambray shirt and a
plain white T-shirt. His Wranglers were also clean
despite being worn through to indecency.

The last time she had a pair of strategically
ripped jeans she'd paid over a hundred dollars for
them. But it had been a long time since she'd been
able to afford clothes costing that much.

He wore work boots. No cowboy boots or
cowboy hat in sight despite him living in the
Cowboy State. A couple U.S. Navy ball caps hung
from the gun rack across the back window, where
he kept his guns under lock and key.

But she'd already glimpsed his not-so-tough
side. He was helping her, wasn't he?

Well, helping to fix her car, at least.

"Do you miss her?" she persisted.

His hesitation made her think he was going
to ignore the question. "I'm only sticking around
long enough to clean up her mess."

His answer wasn't really a yes or a no, but the
kind of response she'd come to expect from him.
"Then what?"

As if trying to see the life ahead of him, he
kept his eye on the road. "Hope someone buys me
out."

"You're not keeping the place?"

"Why would I?"

"Sentimental reasons, I guess." She was under the impression the property had been in the family for a long time, given the comments that had been bandied about in the diner. Something about his granddaddy rolling over in his grave if the grandson sold it.

"Trust me—" he slowed to a crawl, glancing around her before bumping over train tracks "—I don't have a sentimental bone in my body."

That she could believe.

He pulled into the parking lot of an auto parts store in the center of town. "Hard to keep a secret in a place like Henry's Fork, but not a lot of people know about the condition of my mother's house. And I'd appreciate it if they didn't find out."

"Who would I tell?"

He seemed satisfied with her answer. They got out of the truck and he held open the shop's heavy glass door for her. Heads turned as they stepped inside. He pointed her toward the ladies' room and walked up to the counter as if he didn't care that everyone was staring at him.

When she came out a few minutes later a clerk—Jason, according to his name tag—was ringing up the sale. "Thirty-five dollars for the pump," he said. "And five to patch the tire. Just bring it around back."

"That's it?" Angela asked. The amount was half of what she had on her, but less than she'd expected. And a lot less than a new radiator, which was the one thing Hatch had said she didn't need.

While she was still digging around in her purse, he extracted his wallet and paid, ignoring her feeble protest.

"Thank you," she said as the parts technician handed her the boxed pump and receipt. "I'll reimburse you with my next paycheck," she said to Hatch. "Which might be a while."

Since she was out of work at the moment.

He shrugged off her promise. "Do you know how to put that in?"

"If either of you can recommend a good mechanic…?" She glanced from one man to the other. "And where I might find the nearest Western Union office."

Just as soon as she was able, she'd be taking one of those powder puff car maintenance courses like the one she'd seen on the pink flyer in the ladies' room. She never wanted to be this dependent on a man or a mechanic again. She didn't want to be that B movie character in a broken-down car by the side of the road, just waiting for the serial killer to come along.

"Clay should be able to handle a water pump," Jason said. "I'd do it myself just to work on an '80 Seville. Cadillac took a lot of heat that year for using Oldsmobile parts and engines. If it's really pink—" he cast a doubtful eye at Hatch "—I'd be willing to make you an offer."

"Sorry," Angela said. "Shirley signed a contract with Mary Kay. In order to buy the car she had to agree not to sell it to anyone other than a certified GM dealer."

"And GM's required to paint it." Jason shrugged, having known her answer all along. "It was worth a try."

"I'd appreciate it if you could tell me where I might find Clay."

After a moment's hesitation Jason pointed to Hatch.

"Clayton Henry-Miner at your service." Hatch offered a two-finger salute above his eye patch. "Most everyone around here calls me Clay, to my face, at least. A few of my friends, and I do mean few, call me Hatch."

"Guess that makes us friends."

"I wouldn't go that far, darlin'," he said in answer to her cheeky assumption.

She tried not to let his response sting. They'd known each other only a couple of hours or so. A couple of hours in which she'd proposed—and he'd rejected her. That had to count for something.

"Clayton. Is that a family name?" It was kind of old-fashioned. "Is it okay if I still call you Hatch?"

"I'll make an exception."

Her request appeared to amuse him. Good, because she wasn't ready to give up on the whole friendship thing. As in friends helping friends. Convincing him to marry her might be easier if he actually liked her and wanted to help her.

"I'm Angela, by the way. Angela Adams." She finally got around to introducing herself, after having spent some time in the company of a man whose real name she didn't know. And who didn't care enough to ask hers when she'd neglected to mention it. "Now that we've been properly introduced can you please quit calling me darlin'?" She tried imitating his drawl.

"Hardly seems fair. I'm letting you use my tag."

"What does Hatch stand for, anyway?" All this time she'd been thinking Hatch was his last name.

"My friends don't have to ask."

She'd stepped right into that one.

Feeling rather foolish, Angela left the store with the only mechanic in town, aside from Jason, likely to fix her car for free. The guy she knew as Hatch.

Clayton Henry-Miner. The Hermit of Henry's Fork.

Henry, Henry's Fork…

Was there some connection?

Bet he wouldn't tell her that, either.

She held the pump in her lap while they drove around back for the tire. Hatch got out and exchanged a few words with a guy in greasy coveralls. She exited the truck, too, but stayed put while the two men disappeared into the open bay. A short while later Hatch emerged and put her patched tire in back.

"A souvenir." He dropped a coiled horseshoe nail into her palm. Looking at it, she wondered how the curved object had managed to puncture her tire. He nodded toward the courthouse in the town square across the street. "You sure this is what you want?"

It struck her then that he'd bent the nail.

She bit down on her bottom lip. He'd said yes. Yes, with an open-ended symbol that fit perfectly on her ring finger.

She nodded. "I'm sure."

"Marine's don't cry," he pointed out with far

too much sympathy. "At least not any of the Marines I've ever known."

"You're really going to marry me?"

"Either that or take out a restraining order." His lips compressed into a serious line. "I haven't decided yet."

"HUNTING LICENSE?" the middle-aged clerk asked without looking up. "Big game, small game, fur bearing, fowl or waterfowl?"

"The biggest game," Hatch said. "Marriage."

He still hadn't decided against a restraining order. In the short time he'd known her, Peaches had gotten under his skin—and he didn't like anybody crawling around in there. Plus, wouldn't she just love it if she knew he'd tagged her that? Right now the quickest way to end their association appeared to be marriage. She'd be on her way and out of his hair.

And he'd never have to see her again.

The clerk eyeballed him above her reading glasses. "Take a number, please."

Hatch glanced around the empty office. "Carla, you and I are the only ones here."

"Number." She indicated the stand in the middle of the room. Arguing would get him nowhere, so Hatch stepped back and yanked off the next tab.

Carla hit the buzzer beneath her desk and urged the lighted sign. "Forty-two."

"Only three more to go." He waited until she called forty-five before stepping forward. "Forty-five for the month or the year?"

"Don't be a smart-ass, Clay. What brings you to town? Haven't seen you in a while." He'd heard the rumors going around. That he wasn't right in the head since his return from Iraq. That the shrapnel had taken out more than just his eye. That he should have returned sooner, with his mama so sick and all.

That it was too late now for them ever to make amends.

"I'm here for a marriage license," he reminded her.

"I heard you the first time," she said. "And I still don't believe you. Where's your bride?"

"Throwing up in the ladies' room, I suspect."

The woman raised an eyebrow above the rim of her glasses. "Bridal jitters?"

He hoped that was all it was. Outside, Peaches had flung herself at him in a hug so fierce he was still reeling from it. But inside, she'd pressed a hand to her stomach and excused herself to go to the restroom.

"I'd like to get started on the paperwork."

"We'll wait." Carla thrummed her fingernails against the desktop. They didn't have to wait long.

"Sorry," came the familiar refrain.

Carla removed her glasses and glared at him disapprovingly as Angela Adams sidled up beside him. "I'll need to see the bride's ID," Carla said. "She has to be at least eighteen to get married without her parents' permission."

His bride was being carded before she could even fill out the paperwork.

Peaches extended her Colorado driver's license to Carla. "I have my birth certificate and passport if you need them." If he had any doubt that she was serious, the birth certificate and passport squelched it.

With a click of her tongue, the older woman handed him two pens and two clipboards, plus the separated pages of their application, highlighted in pink for her and blue for him.

He passed the pink pages to Angela.

"You okay?" he asked as they sat down in the row of empty chairs to fill out the brief forms. Wyoming had no waiting period for a marriage license. When a cowboy wanted to get hitched, he got hitched.

Without a blood test.

"Yeah."

He looked up to gauge that one-syllable response. She didn't sound okay. "Speak now or forever hold your peace."

She smiled, laughed even. Better.

Except for that nervous edge to her laughter.

"Are you?" She gazed at him anxiously. "Okay with this, I mean?"

He answered with an equal amount of uncertainty. "Yeah."

He'd been saving his first marriage for that first big mistake, and right now he couldn't imagine a bigger one.

She completed her form in record time and handed it to him. He finished his and took both back to the counter, glancing at Angela's vital statistics before turning the forms over to Carla, together with the twenty-five dollar fee and five dollars for the certified copy Angela had said she'd need to give the recruiter once this was all over with. Calhoun owed him big-time.

Hatch glanced at the wall clock and frowned. A quarter to four on a Friday was cutting it close.

"The judge in?" he asked, trying to hurry Carla along.

The sooner they got this over with the better.

She held up an index finger as she talked into the phone, presumably to the judge. "Half his age," she was saying. "And throwing up in the ladies' room."

"I'm standing right here, Carla."

She lowered her voice and craned her neck for a better view of his bride-to-be. "Can't tell if she is or isn't." She covered the mouthpiece. "Is she pregnant?"

"None of your damn business."

With a smug smile, Carla handed over the phone. "Your aunt wants to speak to you."

"She's not half my age," Hatch said in a pre-emptive strike. "Twenty," he responded to the question that followed. "No, she's not pregnant." Not with *his* baby, anyway. "I'm doing a friend a favor. She's a single mom who wants to join the Marine Corps. And that's all there is to it."

Somebody had to sign for her.

He'd finally figured out what Calhoun had known all along. That he was the guy most likely to remember having been dependent on somebody else to join the service.

Parental consent. Spousal support.

Not spousal support in the traditional sense, but he really didn't know what else to call it. Felony? Fraud?

It wasn't as if they were doing this for monetary gain, or even military benefits. He had his own military pension with benefits. And therein lay Calhoun's genius.

Hatch gained nothing by marrying Angela Adams.

Which meant neither of them had anything to lose. As far as he knew, only Immigration Services had a problem with people marrying for the sake of convenience.

Just a signature on a piece of paper.

And here he was, stone-cold sober and ready to sign.

"There's no point in your coming down here," he said to his aunt, when he could get a word in edgewise. The last thing he wanted was his only living relative caught up in this fiasco. "All right." He agreed to stop by later. "See you then."

He handed the phone back to Carla. "You were going to check on the judge," he reminded her.

She took their freshly minted marriage certificate from the printer with her and came back a few minutes later and asked them to wait.

At four o'clock on the dot Carla ushered them

into the wood-paneled chambers of Judge Booker T. Shaw. The judge stood before his massive desk with a Bible and Colt Peacemaker clasped in his hands.

The antique revolver was for show. The cabinet full of rifles behind the desk was not. Every inch of wall space was covered with pictures and plaques of the judge's award-winning bird dogs.

A sign behind his desk read I'd Rather Be Hunting. Judging by the waders beneath his robe and the two Brittany spaniels at his feet, Peaches and Hatch were keeping the man from his preferred pastime.

Hatch could relate. He'd rather be anywhere than here.

Angela stooped to scratch the dogs behind their ears. The judge glanced at her and then at him.

"What's all this nonsense, Clay?" Judge Shaw reviewed the application and license Carla had presented to him, along with whatever commentary the clerk had deemed necessary. So Hatch knew the man had gotten an earful. "Why isn't your aunt here?"

"My aunt couldn't make it," he said. "Just strip it down to the legalese. We don't plan on staying married all that long."

Angela rose to her feet as if expecting the judge

to throw them out. The spaniels wandered off to the rug in front of the unlit fireplace.

"Well, at least you're honest about it. That's more than I can say for most folks." Shaking his head as if he couldn't quite believe what he was about to do, the judge asked his clerk and bailiff to act as witnesses. Carla and Ned stood off to the side nearest the door.

Angela was to Hatch's left, his good-eye side. Where he could see her resolve, which strengthened his. She wanted this paper marriage. And aside from being inconvenienced, he had nothing to lose by giving her what she wanted. Judge Shaw opened the Bible to his cheat sheets and flipped through several before finding the right script. Then he cleared his throat. "We have come together today to witness the marriage of Clay and Angela. The legal requirements of this state having been fulfilled, and the license for their marriage being present, we'll begin."

He raised his eyes from the page to look at them individually. "Clay and Angela, you stand before me having requested that I marry you. Do you both do this of your own free will?"

Angela glanced sideways at Hatch before joining her voice to his. "We do," they answered in unison.

She probably wasn't even aware that in its simplest form marriage was a civil contract between two people. As long as he didn't have to stand here and lie his ass off with promises to love, honor and cherish, he was okay with that.

"Do the witnesses know of any reason we may not legally continue?"

"We do not," Ned replied.

"Your Honor—"

"I said *legally*. Any other reason and I do not want to hear it, Carla. While marriage is never to be entered into lightly, it's up to this young couple to determine what constitutes their marriage. And up to the rest of us to butt out."

The woman shut her mouth.

"Clay, repeat after me," the judge said.

"I do solemnly declare," he repeated, "that I do not know of any lawful impediment why I, Clayton Henry-Miner, may not be joined in matrimony to Angela Anne Adams."

"Angela," the judge prompted.

"I—I do solemnly declare," she said, stumbling over the unfamiliar words, "that I do not know of any lawful impediment why I, Angela Anne Adams, may not be joined in matrimony to Clayton Henry-Miner."

"I take it we're not exchanging rings," the judge said.

Angela twisted the silver knot on her finger—an inspired gesture on Hatch's part. Still a horseshoe nail could not be misconstrued as anything other than what it was. A token meant to wish her luck and send her on her way.

They both responded, "No."

"By the power vested in me by the state of Wyoming—" the judge snapped his Bible shut "—I pronounce you husband and wife." After a few bold strokes of the mighty pen, they entered into that legally binding marriage contract.

"Just so we're clear..." She put the pen down after signing in her pretty penmanship. "I'm keeping my own name."

He'd read her preference on the application. "Wouldn't have it any other way, *darlin'*." She gave him her I-asked-you-nicely-not-to-call-me-that look. Next time, she'd probably not be so nice about it. Fine by him. He'd filled his quota of playing nice for the day.

They left the judge's chambers with her clinging to the marriage certificate she'd driven four hundred miles to obtain. "You hungry?" he asked. "I promised my aunt we'd stop by for dinner."

"The aunt who thinks I'm pregnant?"

"One and the same."

"I'm not pregnant," Angela said to clarify, sparing him a glance as he held the courthouse door for her.

"That's good to know."

CHAPTER THREE

HATCH HAD A QUICK STOP to make before heading over to his aunt's house. He pulled up to a log cabin on the outskirts of town. On the porch a black bear poised to strike wore a rough-hewn wooden sign around its neck with the word Taxidermy burned into it.

After driving around to the garage marked Deliveries, Hatch put the truck into Park. "Wait here. I'll just be a minute," he told her.

"Okay." Her stomach growled a reminder for him not to get sidetracked. He wasn't sure taking her over to aunt's for dinner was such a good idea, but he needed to feed Angela before sending her off on her own again. He shut the door with more force than necessary and went in through the garage.

The air inside was heavy with tanning acids and pickling baths. Big and small game mounting forms and kits covered the walls.

Hatch used the connecting door into the workshop.

Will Stewart looked up from painting the finishing touches on a squirrel. "Was wondering if we'd see you tonight."

"Said I'd try and stop by." Granted, he didn't get to town that often and had been vague about the time when he'd spoken with Stew yesterday, but it wasn't even five o'clock.

"I told Mia she shouldn't believe everything she hears." Stew shoved aside the lighted magnifying glass he used for detail work. Wiping his hands on his apron, he got up from the stool. "There's a rumor going around town that you got married."

"Is that Hatch?"

Before he could even digest that bit of information about the rumor mill, Mia, with little Alex on her hip, was dragging him into a hug as close as the boy and the baby bump would allow. It was good to see her happy again.

"It's true, isn't it?" Stepping back, she looked him over as if to confirm it.

"She's in the truck," he admitted.

"Dammit!" Stew got out his wallet and handed his wife a dollar bill. "You couldn't pick up a phone and call your best friend since second grade?" he muttered as he headed for the door.

"I'm going to get the trophy head and introduce myself to your trophy wife."

Stew stopped in the doorway, shaking his head. "Twenty? Seriously, Hatch. Is that even legal? But it's better than hearing you married a Marine."

"She's not a Marine yet," he qualified. "But we did get married just so she could join."

"Yeah, right." Stew was laughing as he left.

"I'd better go run interference," Hatch said to Mia.

She adjusted little Alex on her hip. "Your wife is in the store."

THE SHOWROOM WAS PACKED floor to ceiling with wall-mounted and freestanding displays. Slowly, Angela turned to absorb it all. She did a double take when Hatch appeared beneath a moose head mounted above an archway.

A pregnant woman carrying a toddler entered behind him. According to their marriage license application, he'd never been married.

But Angela hadn't asked him about a significant other.

"Quite the menagerie you have here." She hoped that hadn't come across quite as awkward as it sounded.

"Welcome to my world," the woman said, a

smile playing at the corner of her generous mouth as she stepped onto the showroom floor. "I'm Mia Stewart, and this is my son, Alex."

"Hi, Alex." Angela zeroed in on the dark-haired, blue-eyed child. "I have a little boy at home about your age." The tot buried his face in his mother's shoulder and then turned to peek again at Angela from beneath spiky lashes. He was a heartbreaker, all right.

"You must be the bride we've heard talk about." Mia paused expectantly.

Angela glanced at Hatch. How was she supposed to respond to that? Surely he didn't want people calling her his bride, when future ex-wife was more appropriate. How much simpler if they'd been able to keep the marriage a secret.

"Angela Adams," she said, introducing herself to the other woman.

Or *as* the other woman?

She hoped she wasn't creating a headache for him.

Chimes rang as a chubby guy in a paint-stained apron entered through the front door. They all pivoted toward him.

"Couldn't find her—" He spotted Angela and stopped. "Hello." He turned accusing eyes on Hatch as he approached her.

"Will Stewart," he said in introduction. "If you're Hatch's bride, then why wasn't I his best man? And how come he never mentioned you?"

Angela really didn't know how to answer that. *Because we just met?*

"No, seriously. How come?"

"I'd love to hear the story," Mia said. "You're welcome to join us for dinner." She grabbed the baby monitor from the counter.

Hatch checked his watch. "My aunt's expecting us."

"Some other time, then," Mia offered. "Angela, it was nice meeting you. Hatch has our number. Maybe we can get the boys together for a play date. And by boys I mean the four of them, so we can have time for some girl talk. I know *all* his secrets, dating back to high school."

Will pointed at himself. "Second grade," he bragged in a stage whisper.

"Afraid Angela's headed back to Denver tonight," Hatch said. "We've got to get going. I'll be dropping off the meat as soon as it's cured."

"You're not leaving without your eye, are you?" his friend demanded.

"I'll stop by next week sometime."

"It's ready now," Will insisted. "Won't take but a minute for me to get it."

"You sell prosthetic eyes?" Angela studied the animals on display. In particular the glass eyes, which were incredibly realistic. "For humans?"

"For Hatch." Will chuckled.

"Will's a third-generation glassblower," Mia bragged, while bouncing the fourth generation on her hip. Alex didn't look much like his dad. But he looked more like a combination of his mom and dad than he did Hatch. That was a relief. Maybe he would grow up to be a glassblowing taxidermist. "Eyes are his specialty."

"But I thought prosthetic eyes were made of silicone." Angela looked to Hatch. He might not be an expert, but he had to know a little something about it.

"Silicone is more durable," Will said. "But you can't beat glass for appearances. Wait here?" he asked Hatch.

He nodded, but didn't look pleased.

Folding her arms, Angela looked around, following Will and Mia with her gaze as they walked off. "Which is more comfortable?"

"You did not just ask me that," he said.

"Sorry." She shifted her eyes back to him. "I didn't mean to make you uncomfortable. What are you wearing right now?"

"Why does this conversation remind me of a dirty phone call?"

Now that she knew he had a sense of humor, she could appreciate the subtlety of it. "So you wear nothing under that patch?"

"Didn't you ever hear curiosity killed the cat?" He inclined his head toward a stuffed mountain lion. Or so she thought, until she saw the domesticated kitty curled up near the lion's paw.

To her relief the *kitty* got up and stretched.

"It's not like I asked you how you lost your eye. I mean, that would be rude, wouldn't it? And I just assumed…" She looked down at her feet. "Because you were a Navy SEAL, it was a battlefield injury."

"Silicone," he said. "An empty socket isn't all that comfortable. I caught a piece of shrapnel in the eye."

"So why do you need the patch?"

"It's practical." He didn't elaborate.

Will returned with a hinged case about the size of one for glasses, which he handed to Hatch. Angela got a peek inside when he opened it. She couldn't believe the fine detail Will had achieved in the cobalt coloring and veining. The artisan beamed with pride as Hatch nodded in appreciation.

"What's the suction cup thingy for?"

Hatch frowned at her. "When are you leaving?"

"As soon as you feed me and fix my car." Her stomach growled on cue.

"Then I guess we'd better get going."

Saying goodbye to the Stewarts, Angela plugged Mia's number into her cell phone, though a play date for Alex and Ryder was doubtful. She wouldn't be in these parts much longer. Still, she didn't really have all that many friends after having dropped out of high school pregnant. It was always nice to add someone to her social network.

Hatch held the truck door for her. "What's so funny?" he asked when she gave a nervous laugh.

"Nothing," she said, tucking her phone away. Mia had just sent a text explaining the suction cup, which was used to position the glass eye and remove it.

"You do know you're damn inconvenient for a marriage of convenience."

A SHORT WHILE LATER THEY pulled up in front of a turn-of-the-century brick Victorian with a powder-blue roof and beige, blue and white gingerbread trim. The plaque beside the door declared the place a historical landmark, while the sign out front identified it as Maddie's Boarding House. Est. 1829

Nowhere near as old as the establishment, Hatch's aunt Maddie met them at the door. She wore colorful layers of loose crinkle skirts and cotton shirts. Angela wouldn't have been surprised to find a crystal ball somewhere in the house.

Maddie held her at arm's length, looking her over from top to bottom. "I thought you said she was pregnant."

"I said no such thing and you know it."

"Wishful thinking on my part, then." Maddie returned her attention to Angela. "Welcome! Never mind me. It's my job to give the boy a hard time. Thirty is a good age for a man to settle down and start a family."

Thirty. That's how old he was.

His aunt ushered them inside. Where Judge Booker T. Shaw was seated at the dining room table. He stood and nodded as they entered the room. "Clay, Angela."

Hatch didn't seem all that surprised to find the judge at his aunt's. Which would explain why he hadn't been afraid to tell the judge exactly what he'd wanted in the way of a wedding ceremony.

She, on the other hand, had prepared herself for

the "to have and to hold" version, justifying this in her mind as words said every day by people who later regretted them. She felt relieved not to have entered into that lie.

Especially now that she'd come face-to-face with the judge again. "Your Honor."

"Judge will do, Ms. Adams."

"Angela, please."

"I hope you're hungry." Maddie showed Angela where to wash up, and had her seated by the time Hatch came down the stairs a few minutes later.

He'd done more than just wash up. He'd trimmed his beard and pulled back his hair. What couldn't be pulled back fell in damp waves around his face. He still wore his eye patch. Which meant what?

He didn't like his new eye? Or was he just that self-conscious? He didn't seem like the self-conscious type.

For whatever reason, he chose to present an in-your-face tough-guy image to the world. Which left her to conclude that the patch covered the vulnerability she'd glimpsed earlier and not just his prosthetic eye.

"So, Angela," Maddie said as she sat next to the judge. "I'd say you went above and beyond the call of duty to join the Marines."

Hatch was the one who'd gone above and beyond. "I just did what I had to."

"Be sure to tell Calhoun I'll be collecting," Hatch said. "From him, not from you."

He must have added that qualification because he'd seen the look of panic in her eyes. She didn't like being indebted. And she knew he would come away with nothing from their arrangement except being lighter by a few dollars. Which she intended to pay back.

Before helping himself, he passed the bread basket from Maddie to her.

"Thank you." Angela set a homemade roll on her plate.

She couldn't recall the last time she'd sat down for a meal like this. Must have been that last Thanksgiving with her parents. And here it was not even a week away from that holiday.

"What made you choose the military?" the judge asked.

"My dad got his start in the Navy as a photographer and went on to make a career of it after he got out." She broke the crusty roll in half as Hatch passed her the butter.

"Explains why you tried the Navy first." She shouldn't be surprised he remembered that from their earlier conversation. "You can choose any branch of the service."

"Said the Navy man." She wondered if he missed it. Her father had always spoken of his service with pride. "I didn't choose the Marine Corps—it chose me." The Navy recruiter had seen a single mom. The Marine recruiter saw beyond the single mom to what she wanted to be.

"What does your mother do?" Maddie asked.

"She was a volcanologist. Both my parents were killed in a plane crash four years ago." Angela took her time spreading butter on the roll. She hadn't been on board, but hadn't flown in a plane since.

"I'm so sorry, dear." Maddie touched Hatch's forearm as if he'd pass her sincerity along, the way he did the meatball stroganoff and the green beans.

He didn't reach out to her. But Angela shrugged off the sympathy just the same. Normally the platitudes "at least they died together" or "at least they died doing what they loved" followed such expressions of condolence. All that meant was she'd lost both parents.

"I was homeschooled until high school. A family vacation for us was a trip to Yosemite to see the supervolcanoes. That's where my folks met. She was working on her master's thesis and he was shooting a coffee table book."

Angela speared several green beans with her fork. "They never did get married. But they were together almost two decades."

They'd loved each other. And they'd loved her.

But any stability in her life had come from Shirley, because her parents didn't always take her with them. After they'd died, her grandmother had insisted on enrolling her in a public high school. Of course, that hadn't turned out so hot.

Angela slanted a glance toward Hatch, who appeared to be digesting more than just his dinner, even though he didn't comment. Not that her parents were opposed to marriage, but she wondered what they would have said about her reason for marrying him.

Did it matter? She'd gotten what she wanted. "Shirley—that's my grandmother," she said for Maddie's and the judge's benefit, "says I inherited a restless heart. Which is why I can't hold a job."

"You're only twenty." Hatch frowned. "You have plenty of time to figure out what you want in a career."

"I still have a responsibility to Ryder." She met Maddie's sympathetic gaze across the table. "The military is my chance to do something with my life while providing some stability for my son. It's a start, anyway."

"I'd love to see some pictures of your little one," the older woman said.

"After dinner," Hatch suggested when Angela reached for the cell phone beside her plate.

He wasn't much of a conversationalist, and she'd already said too much. But Maddie more than made up for it with engaging family anecdotes.

Maddie was his paternal aunt, his father's sister.

She'd never married, never had any children.

Though she doted on her nephew, obviously.

Hatch had a room upstairs. But he preferred to "rough it." Whatever that meant. And Maddie had no other tenants, because they were too much bother and got in the way of her restoration work. According to Maddie she'd inherited a money pit.

The judge was a family friend and frequent dinner guest. And Maddie hinted at romance there. He'd likewise never married.

"My great-great-great-grandfather had this house built for his mistress," Maddie said. "Rumor has it she ran it as a brothel. The first Maddie Miner was their illegitimate daughter, who turned it into a more respectable boarding house."

Leaning over her plate, Angela listened to Maddie carry on about the Miners' colorful history.

"The Henrys, in contrast, were the salt of the earth," Hatch said with a touch of familial sarcasm. "Founding fathers. Land owners. Six generations of cattlemen."

"Don't let him fool you." Maddie used her fork for emphasis. "That side of the family had quite a few outlaws and bandits."

They bantered over which family had the more infamous characters. As Angela saw it, Hatch won either way, being a member of both. But he seemed to identify more with the Henrys.

Maybe because of his namesake.

If there was one member he considered the salt of the earth, clearly, it was his grandfather.

"This house was passed to me around the time my brother, Matt, went to work for Clayton Henry," Maddie said. "Isabella Henry was a rare beauty and Matthew could be real a charmer. Those two were on a collision course from the moment they met."

The man between them tensed.

"It's a shame everything fell apart after." Maddie adjusted the napkin in her lap and patted her nephew's arm. "Lots of good times before the bad. And I see the best of both of them in Clay."

"You still planning on putting Two Forks up for sale?" the judge asked.

"I have more work to do around the place, but yes," Hatch replied.

"What's your asking price?"

"One point three."

"In this economy? Why wouldn't you hold on to the property? You're not going to get that, and it's worth twice as much. Bennett's place is listed dirt cheap and has been on the market three years."

"Bennett doesn't have two forks of the river running through it, two pine groves, the peach orchard. And I could go on about the outbuildings."

"All of which are in disrepair," the judge argued. "He's got just as much acreage in meadowland."

"I'm sure Clay's thought of all that," Maddie said, coming to her nephew's defense. "You can't bully him into keeping it, Booker."

"I'm not trying to bully anyone. It's just a shame the land was ever parceled out. But, Clay—" the judge returned his attention to Hatch

"—you could take what's left and make something of it."

"Sometimes a person just has to let go," Maddie said.

"Then answer me this." The judge used his fork to emphasize his point. "If he's so eager to let go, why hasn't he?"

"There's still work to be done," Hatch said.

Angela didn't know what to make of their heated debate. Most of what was said went over her head. But it wasn't as if the two men were angry with each other. Just opinionated.

"Call a cleaning company," the judge continued. "Have the house cleared out in a couple of days, instead of spending all your damn time holed up at the ranch, chasing people off the property. Which is going to land you in my courtroom," he warned.

"Booker, you make him sound like his mother," Maddie said with a nervous laugh. "He didn't make that mess."

"No, the judge is right," Hatch said, springing to the man's defense. "It is my mess. It always was."

Angela didn't interpret this as a confession of a secret life of slovenliness. So why was he accepting responsibility?

"If you don't want to live in your mother's house, the foundation was laid for a new house a long time ago," the judge said. "Build on that."

The conversation seemed to have taken an uncomfortable turn for Hatch with the mention of his mother and the house. He focused on his plate. She bumped his knee underneath the table, causing him to look at her in question.

Accident? Or on purpose?

She bumped him again as he held her gaze. Although they'd had their awkward moments today, Angela saw this as *her* chance to rescue *him* for a change.

"These Swedish meatballs are delicious," she said, taking another bite.

Maddie went into detail about the recipe, as Angela had been hoping she would, starting with stale bread and sour milk.

Angela stopped chewing when the woman got to venison.

Deer meat? Just like the deer carcass they'd left swinging from a tree while they'd dropped off his head to be mounted and sold.

"Are you planning on bow hunting this season?" The judge trod on neutral ground. "What are you doing about a kill plot?"

"Kill plot?" Angela looked at Hatch and swallowed. Then took a big gulp of water to wash down the meatball stuck in her throat.

"Seeded area that draws the deer to the hunter." His answer was matter-of-fact.

She blanched. "I feel like I've landed in an episode of *Kill It, Cook It, Eat It*."

"That's about right." He took pity on her and stabbed the last meatball on her plate, then brought it to his mouth with the hint of a smile.

Angela sighed. "After today, I'm seriously thinking of becoming a vegan."

THEY CLEARED THE TABLE and loaded the dishwasher together. Well, he did. She just got in his way.

Hatch tossed the dish towel over his shoulder and turned his back to the sink. "What's so funny?" Aside from her talking about becoming a vegan—after she'd polished off a plate of Maddie's meatballs.

"Nothing," she said, distracted by her cell phone. "I'm sorry. Do you need my help with anything?"

"Who is it you keep texting on that thing?"

"Why is it you don't have one?"

Because he'd spent thirteen years as a Navy

SEAL, living for the adrenaline rush a phone call could bring.

Wheels up. Hooyah!

"I don't see the need for one."

He wanted to work some things through without distractions from the outside world. Aside from the occassional odd job, he'd been in seclusion for the past fifteen months. The past three back at the ranch. The judge had called him on that at dinner. Hatch had been taking his time cleaning up the property, because that was what he needed to do.

But if what he was really doing was guarding his mother's treasures... Well, then he was, in fact, just like her. Or it was taking him a lot longer than he'd imagined to work through his grief and guilt.

"Boyfriend?" he pressed as her thumbs moved across the screen.

"Yeah, I have a boyfriend and a *husband*."

"In name only. You can have as many boyfriends as you want."

"It's my new BFF, Mia," Angela confessed, putting the phone away. "I have a kid. A seventy-seven-year-old grandmother. And until recently two jobs. When would I have time for a boyfriend?"

"You're going to want that divorce sooner than you think," Hatch replied. "Just make sure he's one of the good guys and has a couple years and a couple pay grades on you."

"Are you giving me dating advice?"

Hatch hung the dish towel on the oven door. "Something else to keep in mind," he said, moving to the refrigerator for a beer. "When a military man says he's separated, he could be talking geography."

"You're serious?"

"And stay away from Special Ops." He twisted the cap of his beer and gestured with the bottle.

She choked back a laugh. "Aren't you a Special Ops guy?"

"Divorce rates are higher," he noted as a matter of practicality. "Assuming you plan to do this only one more time."

"How is it you made it to thirty and never married?"

"Marriage is no guarantee of anything," he said.

But he figured that someday she'd want the kind of commitment that was supposed to be part of the package. And as far as he was concerned, the sooner he got her off his hands the better. Because Jessie hadn't been far from his thoughts today, he couldn't help the protective surge he felt sending Angela out into the worldwide web of military men.

Maddie stepped into the kitchen just then. "Should we have dessert in the dining room? Or is it cozier here in the kitchen?"

"I couldn't eat another bite," Angela protested as Hatch's aunt got out the serving plates for her famous peach pie. "Thank you for your hospitality, but I really need to get going."

"We can't let you drive all that way tonight. Clay?" His aunt turned to him for backup. "Talk some sense into this girl."

BENEATH THE METALLIC-PINK hood of the Cadillac, Angela watched as Hatch switched out the water pump. Daylight faded to the west in pretty ribbons of orange and blue.

"Back home they call that Bronco sky. For the Denver Broncos." With the fading light came a drop in temperature, and she shoved her hands deeper into her vest pockets. "Do you follow football at all?"

He glanced over his shoulder toward the sunset. "Means a cold snap is coming."

"Did you play in high school?" she persisted.

"Didn't have time for sports." This time when

he looked up, he peered over at her. "Feel free to wait in the truck."

He'd left his vehicle running, with the high beams shining on the car, doors open—and radio booming a mix of pop rock, hip-hop and contemporary country. His taste in music seemed as eclectic as his skills.

"I'm fine." She ignored the hint with a touch of guilt. He didn't need her as a distraction. His fingers were probably numb from the cold. "Think we'll get snow tonight? Bad enough to close the interstate?"

In which case she really would be stuck in Wyoming. If she left no later than seven o'clock, she still had a chance to make it home tonight before Shirley missed her. Angela had been vague with her grandmother about this thing she had to do. She'd told her she'd be gone all day, and probably home late that night.

Because she really didn't want Shirley to stop her.

"You really should consider staying in town tonight."

They'd had this discussion back at his aunt's house, and both he and Maddie had valid points. But as tired as Angela was, she just wanted to get home. Kiss her son good-night, and fall into her own bed.

She clamped her chattering teeth together while Hatch went back to work on the pump. The only real warm spot seemed to be right next to him. She stood as close as she dared, bouncing on her toes, twitching in time to Ke$ha. *We R Who We R.*

He stopped tinkering. The socket wrench stilled in his hand. This time when he straightened to his full height, he set the tool aside with a heavy sigh and leaned against the Caddy.

She stopped dancing. "What? I didn't say a word."

He wiped his hands on the dirty rag she'd used to surrender with, and tossed it aside. "Oh, you were talking, all right."

He dropped the hood with a thunk and handed her the keys.

"You're done?" It had taken him all of twenty minutes to change out the water pump. Even with her as a distraction.

"That should get you home. Car needs an overhaul," he added, more to himself than to her. He put the old pump in the box, picked up his tools and carried them back to his truck. "You have

Maddie's number?" Returning, he opened her car door for her.

Angela stepped forward. "I'll be fine." She drew him into an awkward hug that he didn't seem to know how to return. "Thank you."

"It's been an interesting few hours, Angela Adams."

She climbed behind the wheel, but couldn't shut the door because he stood there with one arm across the top of the window and the other on the roof. "I'm going to follow you to the state line," he said.

"That's crazy." Cheyenne was, like, a ten-hour round trip for him.

"No, crazy is letting you drive off in this piece of crap, down a lonely stretch of highway, and having the sheriff show up at my door tomorrow because you didn't make it home."

"You really are a worst-case-scenario thinker, aren't you?"

ANGELA ARRIVED HOME well after midnight, with ten pounds of venison and Maddie's Swedish meatball recipe. Once inside the small apartment, she headed straight to the kitchen and shoved the meat into the freezer.

If only she could put her emotions in cold

storage that easily. The drive home had been physically exhausting. The entire day had been emotionally draining. And it wasn't over yet.

"Angela Anne Adams!" Shirley got up from the couch, where she'd been dozing off in front of the TV. Angela came and went at odd hours for work, so there was only one reason for her grandmother to use that tone of voice with her. "Where have you been?"

Ryder reached for her from his playpen.

He was wide-awake, with red marks where his cheek had rested on the mattress. A light sleeper, like his mother, he was often up when she got home from work.

"I had something to do." She picked up her son and moved down the hall toward the bathroom.

Shirley followed. "Your boss called about your last paycheck. I know you got fired."

Angela had been a desk clerk at night and worked in housekeeping during the day for a small resort, until she'd fallen asleep on the job during a double shift. "Can we not talk about this now? I'm really tired."

"That's always your excuse."

"That's because I'm always tired." She was even too tired to find anything amusing about Shirley's bright orange hair in those dated pink rollers. "Could we have a real Thanksgiving dinner this year?"

"What's the matter with Denny's?"

"I'll cook," Angela volunteered, looking down at her son, but speaking to her grandmother. She could put off becoming a vegan until after the holidays. Until tonight she hadn't even realized she'd been depriving her son of that family tradition.

"Is something wrong? You know you can tell me anything."

"Don't worry." She thought of those flashing headlights in her rearview mirror on the outskirts of Cheyenne, where Hatch had let her know she'd continue on her own. "Everything will be all right from here on out."

"Oh," Shirley said, as if she'd forgotten to mention something. "A Marine recruiter called this afternoon. Said he was passing a message along from someone named Hatch." She lifted an eyebrow, though the surprise was on Angela. "Tell your *friend* Hatch thank-you for letting me know you were safe with him in Wyoming."

Angela turned beet-red. She said good-night to her grandmother, glad to have that out in the open.

"You're getting heavy." She turned her attention to Ryder. Sat him on the closed toilet seat while she ran warm water over a clean washcloth. She wrung it out and he held up a grubby hand with a candy heart that said Be Mine.

"Where did you find that?" She cringed. "The couch cushions?" That candy had to be left over from Valentine's Day, or, more likely, an after Valentine's Day clearance.

"Nana," he said.

"Oh, Nana Shirley." Who needed to be scolded. And then it would be Angela's guilt trip, because she hadn't been here. And because she relied too heavily on her grandmother for her son's care. Some days she felt like the worst mother.

"You eat." He shoved it at her.

"You know just how to fix my broken heart, don't you?"

His smile lit up her night.

CHAPTER FOUR

Six Months Later

HATCH DROPPED THE PENCIL to the legal pad. "Thought she was supposed to be here by now." Never mind that he'd canceled his trip to Cairo, Egypt, so that he would be. He could have used the infusion of cash that job would have given him.

He ran a hand through his short hair, still not used to having a military cut again. He'd hate to admit he'd cleaned himself up after he found out she was coming.

"Your impatience is showing."

The kitchen timer went off and his aunt pushed herself up from the dining room table. She patted his shoulder as she went to take the cookies out of the oven.

"It's these damn numbers giving me a headache." He rubbed the bridge of his nose, then below his eye patch. The ranch had been on the market for six months now without a single offer. The thought of lowering the asking price again killed him.

His aunt walked back in and set a plate of peanut butter cookies in front of him—his favorite. She'd been baking all morning in anticipation of their guests' arrival.

Guests, my ass.

"Thanks." He ignored the cookies and went back to his calculations, none of which made any sense at this point. He scratched out the bottom line and pushed the legal pad aside, along with the plate of cookies.

Years of supplementing his mother's income on a military paycheck had put him behind financially. Since his return to Two Forks Ranch less than a year ago, he'd already spent close to $30K in back taxes and cleaning up the property. Another $15,600 in property taxes would be due in October unless he came up with a price low enough to interest someone into taking the place off his hands.

He didn't need the money as much as he needed to sell the property. He got by on his monthly military pension. Any money he made from the sale of the ranch would be for retirement. So why was he wrestling with dropping the price?

As if he had a reason for wanting to hold on to Two Forks.

Maddie angled the pad toward her for a better look. "What's this?"

Along with the new listing price, he'd been working through another problem that didn't quite add up. His grandpa Henry had always said it took twenty acres of Wyoming scrub for every two cows, although conventional wisdom put that number at more like ten. There just wasn't enough acreage left. At least, not for the operation the ranch had once been.

But if Hatch could make enough to pay the property taxes year after year, it might be worth holding out until the economy turned around. Which the economists were saying could take another eight or nine years. He just had to determine his break-even point. And maybe he could even turn a profit if he increased the herd to the hundred and twenty or so head the ranch could sustain.

"Didn't Grainger offer to sell you a dozen weaned calves? It'd be a start."

"Not sure I'm up to losing the place all over again."

"You were fifteen," his aunt said. "Quit beating yourself up. The responsibility wasn't yours to begin with."

"It'd be at least two years before I could turn a profit on a calf." But what else was he going to do with his time?

He'd been forced to retire from the military at thirty.

"Call the real estate agent and take the property off the market," Maddie said, pulling her cell phone out of her pocket and handing it to him. "At least while you're thinking about it. You'll sleep better."

Hatch punched in the agent's number. There was another reason now was not a good time to sell, and they both knew it. Just last week he'd been adding those personal touches that would make the house a home.

He was in the middle of his conversation with the agent when he spotted Angela through the lace panel over the window in the front door. He stood up to conclude his business.

"I've got it." His aunt opened the door before Angela even had the chance to knock. "Look at you, as pretty as ever," Maddie was saying. "And this must be Ryder. What a big boy you are."

Maddie bent to fuss over the youngster, and Hatch caught Angela's gaze over their heads. To her credit, she could still look him in the eye after appointing him her son's guardian.

"Ryder, this is Aunt Maddie," she said in introduction. "And this is Mommy's friend Hatch. You remember me telling you about him, don't you?"

The three-year-old nodded.

Hatch and the red-haired boy stared at each other with nothing much to say. Little kid. Big responsibility.

Maddie took matters in hand. "Your mom tells me peanut butter cookies are your favorite." The boy nodded and she ushered him into the kitchen for a glass of milk and cookies.

"Hatch." Angela crossed her arms, acknowledging him with a wariness in her eyes that hadn't been there before.

She'd grown up some in the past six months. For one thing, she wasn't that skinny kid anymore. She'd put on a good ten pounds of lean muscle in boot camp. And the tilt of her chin was confident rather than defiant.

He'd kept tabs on her through Calhoun. She'd enlisted in the Marine Corps as soon as she'd returned to her home state. Made it all the way through boot camp to earn her Eagle, Globe and Anchor as a Marine.

He could see that in the way she carried herself.

Even in that breezy top and cropped jeans.

The last time he'd seen her he'd been filling up her car at the pump for her trip home. After boot camp she'd sent him a polite thank-you note with a check for a hundred dollars for "expenses incurred" the day he'd married her. That was one way of putting it.

But no mention of when it would be *convenient* for them to get that divorce.

"I'm sorry," she said. Now there was a familiar refrain. "There was one else for me to ask."

And here she was, apologizing to him. Because the only reason she was here at all was to use him *again.*

He should say something in the way of condolences at her grandmother's passing. He'd had to hear about it through Maddie.

Apparently, Angela and his aunt, and Mia, for that matter, were Facebook friends. Which was the only reason he had even secondhand information about her.

"I'm expected back in three days. They gave me only ten days' emergency leave, and the funeral arrangements and travel here took up most of that."

"Sorry to hear about your grandmother." There.

He'd forced those first words out. Things had to get easier after that.

"Thank you for the flowers."

He inclined his head.

He didn't know anything about any flowers. That must have been Maddie's doing. Though she'd probably mentioned it to him. Probably even charged the flowers to his account. But he was so shell-shocked after learning Angela had named him her boy's guardian.

He didn't know what to think.

"I have some papers for you to sign." She reached down for her folder at the same time he did. Their hands touched and she pulled back.

Well, she still had something soft about her even if she was now a Marine. But he shouldn't be grabbing for her papers no matter how anxious he was to see what she'd committed him to.

"This can wait," he said, retrieving the folder and handing it to her. He picked up her bag and the boy's Elmo backpack. "I'll take these up to your room."

HE'D STOLEN ALL THE AIR from her lungs, and she wasn't able to breathe again until he left the room. One big deep breath and she was ready to join Maddie and Ryder in the kitchen.

Seeing Hatch shouldn't have been this hard. They'd parted on relatively good terms. Neither of them had tried to remain in contact. And she'd paid him back. But he'd checked up on her through her recruiter.

They'd had an unspoken agreement to respect each other's privacy. Everything would work out in the end with an amicable divorce. But it wasn't as if she'd put having a husband completely from her mind until a couple days ago, when she'd needed him again.

Though she knew that was how it must seem.

"Is he really okay with this?" Angela stood in Maddie's kitchen, nibbling on a cookie. Because of little ears, she stopped herself from saying Hatch looked pissed.

But he did look pissed, good and pissed, to her. If not for that and the eye patch, she wouldn't have even recognized him. His cobalt-blue eye still captured her attention, but with his shorter hair, his face had become the focal point. She'd had no idea that that firm jaw and those set lips even existed.

Let alone that he was handsome.

Maddie smoothed Ryder's hair. "What choice does he have?"

Exactly. Angela hadn't given Hatch one.

She had been all set to deploy to Afghanistan when her grandmother had died of an aneurism, leaving Angela devastated and without a guardian for Ryder.

The military had not only expected her to pick up the pieces of her life in a matter of days, but they'd demanded it. She'd been sitting in the Judge Advocate General's office, not knowing what to do about appointing a new guardian for Ryder, when the JAG officer presented her with the simple solution.

The Navy lawyer—Navy because the Navy and Marine Corps shared legal officers—naturally assumed her lawfully wedded husband, Ryder's stepfather, would take responsibility for her son's care in her absence, and had filled out the paperwork accordingly.

All she had to do was sign.

Heaven help her, she did. Hatch had seemed a better option than the three military families she'd interviewed. Not that they weren't all nice enough and willing to take care of her son for the length of her deployment.

It was just that Hatch and Maddie were family—the only family she and Ryder had left. Based on a marriage that existed on paper only.

Maddie, bless her heart, had been on board from the start.

The only bump in the road had been telling Hatch, after the fact, that he would be responsible for her son in her absence. He didn't have a cell phone or a computer, which made it difficult to get in touch with him except though his aunt.

But those were excuses. Angela knew signing those documents without his knowledge or consent had been wrong. Which was why she was feeling so unsettled now.

Nibbling on another cookie, she wished she'd handled this whole thing differently.

"Mommy?" Ryder crawled out of his chair to tug on the hem of her top. "Can I have another cookie?" he whispered, as though his request was some big secret.

He darted glances at Maddie, too shy to ask her directly. He wasn't the shy type, so all that would change quickly.

A whole year away from her baby.

She crouched to his level. He was an amazingly adaptable kid. But tomorrow she'd be leaving Henry's Fork, and in three days heading for the other side of the world—while he'd be staying in Wyoming with people who were virtual strangers to him.

All this after losing his Nana Shirley.

As tempting as it was to give him anything he wanted right now, she did the parenting thing. "No, you may not. You'll spoil your dinner."

"You had four cookies." He held up four fingers.

Four? Really? She must be nervous if she didn't remember shoving that many cookies into her mouth.

"I'm bigger." She tweaked his nose.

"You ready?" Hatch asked from the doorway. "We have a lot of ground to cover today."

Angela pushed herself to her feet. Despite his not having vowed for better or for worse, she'd once again brought her burdens with her to Wyoming and placed them squarely on the broad shoulders filling the doorway.

Maddie was already using a washcloth on Ryder's face and hands. "We're ready," Angela said, taking her son's clean hand in hers.

"Maybe the boy can stay here," Hatch suggested.

Angela followed his gaze to Maddie's. The woman must have seen the panicked look on her face. "No, he needs to go with the two of you."

Not that Angela didn't want to be alone with Hatch—they'd have to talk things out sooner or later. She just wanted to spend every last minute with her son.

And Ryder needed to get used to his new family. Mostly Hatch, since the man wasn't that easy to get to know. Angela had thought about having Ryder call him Uncle Hatch, to make it easier for her son. But the idea seemed kind of creepy to her.

Hatch was her spouse. And by default, Ryder's stepdad. Yet having her son call him Daddy was totally out of the question.

She'd never explained to Ryder about his real father, let alone that she'd gotten married, and he had a stepdad who didn't live with them. But who he was going to live with now.

Hopefully, she had a couple more years before Ryder started asking those impossible questions about where he'd come from.

Of course, with no man in his young life, ever, there was every risk of Ryder growing very attached to Hatch.

HE'D HITCHED HER U-HAUL to his truck, and she and her son followed in the Caddy. Turning onto the ranch road, Angela noticed first the For Sale sign, and next that the water pump mailbox stood upright, held in place by a tractor tire planted with a bed of colorful petunias.

Meadows were in bloom and water trickled in the creek. The scent of peach blossoms filled the air.

Hatch pulled into the yard and backed the trailer up to the barn, where they'd be offloading her stuff for storage. The thing about being the head of a single-parent household was she'd lost her housing with this deployment. Letting a house on base sit empty for a year wasn't practical for the military.

She'd be able to get back on the waiting list when she returned. But for now Hatch's Wyoming ranch was the closest thing they had to a home.

Angela parked under the cottonwood. Instead of a deer carcass hanging from the tree, there was a tire swing, low enough to the ground for a three-year-old boy to climb on and play. *Thank you, Hatch.*

Everything about the place had changed, yet seemed so familiar. The house had a fresh coat of light blue paint and new, darker blue shutters. No more cracked or broken windows.

The wire fencing was straight and the wooden fencing sturdy. Metal buildings had been power

sprayed and those made out of wood painted. The
only things missing were farm animals. Ranch
hands to take care of them. And an owner who'd
appreciate all the hard work Hatch had so obviously put into the place. Not for the first time she
wondered why he'd even consider selling. He belonged here.

Meanwhile, the man who'd agreed to care for
her son while she was away—maybe *acquiesced*
was a better word—exited his truck and walked
around to the back of the U-Haul and he started
to unload.

Ryder had drifted to sleep on the short ride.
Angela got out of the car and opened the back
door, but waited for him to stir instead of waking
him.

The drive from California to Wyoming had
been a long one. Because of her time constraints,
she'd driven the thousand miles in two days. And
he'd already slept most of this one away.

They'd both be paying a price later tonight.

After lifting Ryder out of his car seat, she set
him on his feet, and they walked hand in hand
toward Hatch, who was making short work of un-
loading her few possessions.

Though she imagined most of Ryder's care
would be handled by his doting aunt Maddie,

Angela knew she'd made the right decision in choosing Hatch, a Silver Star recipient, over a foster family.

She'd researched him on Google. That was how she'd learned of his Silver Star. The gold star with the tiny Silver Star at its center was the third highest combat decoration. Awarded for gallantry in action. In his case, facing down the enemy while badly injured. She'd asked Calhoun about it. All he'd said was that it was well deserved. And that she should ask Hatch.

Maybe someday she would.

And other awards. Too many to name. That brief online glimpse into his military career and her day trip to Wyoming six months ago were the total of everything she knew about him. Yet he was the person she trusted most to look after her son.

He looked up as she approached with her little one in tow. "I've got this," he said. "Have you been inside yet?"

She shook her head.

"It's safe to use the bathroom."

"I have to go potty," Ryder said on cue.

"Then we'd better check it out." She smiled to herself as she and Ryder headed inside, remembering the last time she'd been in this house to use the bathroom. That Hatch was joking with her was a good sign.

The house had a new screen door, and the front door was unlocked. She stopped just inside, amazed how different the place was.

It wasn't just clean, but empty. A fresh coat of paint in a neutral beige covered the walls throughout. No doubt the real estate agent's suggestion. The downstairs was all hardwood floors and area rugs, with the walls between the family room, dining room and kitchen knocked out to form one big open space.

Only the den, through a wide arched doorway, was separate.

The kitchen was a total remodel, with stainless-steel appliances and new cabinets and countertops.

A butcher-block table with high-back chairs for a family of six formed a dining area near the kitchen. And a seating area off to one side had a couch, an armchair and accent tables.

Accessories were tasteful. The place looked nice, but staged, as if no one lived there.

"Mommy," Ryder whined.

"Okay." They trudged upstairs and straight to the bathroom, which wasn't hard to find.

The second floor was carpeted wall to wall in

soft beige. The agent had done a good job making sure the house looked contemporary without that ultramodern feel that would be wasted on a rustic place like this.

The first thing she noticed coming out of the bathroom was that the master bedroom across the hall appeared lived in. She peeked through the door and was surprised to find that Hatch seemed to sleep here, at least part of the time.

The bed had been made, though in a hurry.

A pair of running shoes lay near a chair, with running shorts draped over the arm. A change jar and other personal items sat on the dresser.

"Have you picked out your room yet?" Hatch startled her, but he was talking to Ryder.

"This one," her son said.

"No, this one's mine," Hatch replied, leading them down the hall to a corner room. "How about this one?"

Ryder's eyes popped. But he couldn't have been any more surprised than Angela was. "I thought..."

She didn't know how to finish without Ryder catching on that the move was more permanent.

As in a whole year.

"Maddie's place is a museum," Hatch said. "A boy needs room to run around, and if I'm going to be responsible for him, he's going to stay under my roof."

"But the For Sale sign out front?"

"I've changed my mind."

She glanced at him again. He'd changed his mind because of her situation. Could she be any more of an imposition?

Ryder turned and pressed himself against her legs, all shy again. Peering up at her with expectant eyes, he whispered, "Is this my room, Mommy?"

The only room in the house that wasn't beige, it was decorated like a Marvel comic book. With wall posters and superhero accents around the room. In one corner spidy web kept stuffed toys off the ground. A night-light beamed the bat signal to the ceiling.

Green Lantern bedside lamps.

Captain American drawer pulls.

Ironman bedding.

The new-paint smell was stronger in here, as if the vertical blue stripes that seemed to bring it all together had just been added.

Like, in the past seven days, after Grandma Shirley had died and Angela had explained her dilemma to Maddie, then let his aunt explain it to Hatch.

One entire wall was done in blackboard paint—magnetized blackboard paint. Brightly colored alphabet magnets spelled out small words a three-year-old might recognize, like CAT and HAT.

Numbers. 1+2=3.

And someone had written Ryder's Room in chalk.

Angela smoothed back Ryder's hair. "Yes, I guess it is."

"Yipee!" The décor was a little "old" for a boy his age. But that didn't stop Ryder from running over to the bed and jumping on it.

"Hey, no monkey," she said, plucking him up.

He continued to bounce in her arms. "'No more monkeys jumping on the bed,'" he said, quoting one of his favorite picture books. She hoped Hatch would read to him. She'd miss that cuddle time with her son.

Hard to imagine Hatch cuddling.

"That's right," she said, putting him down. "Tell Hatch thank you."

Ryder walked over to him and tugged on his shirtsleeve. "Mr. Hatch," he said, looking what must seem like a long way up. "Where's Mommy's room?"

"You want your mom to have a room?" Hatch met her gaze above Ryder's head and nodded. She certainly hadn't given her son the idea. She hadn't even known about this room.

"There's one across the hall," Hatch said to Ryder. "And one down the hall on the other side of the bathroom, across from mine. You decide."

Ryder scurried from one room to the other and back again. Both were empty for the most part, but one had a rocking chair, and a crib frame filled with collectible porcelain dolls. All of them had black hair and blue eyes. Ryder seemed to weigh the proximity of the presence against the rocking chair in the other.

He ran back for another look at the other room.

"This was my sister, Jessie's, room," Hatch said, standing in the doorway while Angela looked around. This room and the other had the same neutral paint as the rest of the house. "She died of SIDS. Those dolls are what's left of my mother's collection—the start of her hoarding." He shoved his hands deep into this pockets. "They all look like Jessie. I'm having a hard time getting rid of them for that reason."

Angela couldn't imagine what it was like to lose a sister, a baby. Her heart melted as she looked at him.

Her son squeezed past Hatch and into the room.

"This one." Ryder climbed up on the wooden

rocker and, feet dangling, used his little body to set the chair in motion.

"We can move the rocker to the other room," Hatch offered.

"No, this room's bigger," Ryder said with finality.

"Only if it's okay with your mom."

Ryder jumped from the chair and beamed up at her. "Do you like this room or the other room?"

What was Hatch doing? She wouldn't need a room. She wasn't even going to be here. But she played along. "No, this one's fine."

"Okay." Hatch crouched to Ryder's level. "We'll fix it up nice while your mom's gone."

No, no, no! She hadn't said anything to Ryder yet about leaving. Better to take these things one step at a time at his age. He was already overwhelmed by Shirley's death, the funeral, packing up the house…

The drive to Wyoming.

Meeting family he didn't know he had.

She wasn't ready to check "Mom's leaving" off the list yet.

"Are you leaving again, Mommy?" Ryder's lower lip trembled. She crouched as Hatch stood up.

"Yes, I am. Is that okay?" Those thirteen weeks in boot camp had felt like a lifetime.

On the verge of tears, he shook his head. "Nooo."

She was about to pull him into a hug. Of course it wasn't okay. What kind of mother was she, leaving her baby? And yet, this was what she'd signed up for.

"Of course it's okay." Hatch put a firm hand on her son's shoulder and led him toward the stairs. "Your mom has an important job to do for the Marine Corps. And you and me have the important job of fixing up her room for her while she's gone."

Angela straightened and followed them halfway down the stairs before realizing Ryder wasn't crying.

CHAPTER FIVE

OUTSIDE, HATCH SPENT A FEW more minutes distracting the boy with the tire swing. Or maybe distracting himself as he pushed. He didn't know why he'd told Angela about his sister. He'd just thought she should know in case Ryder picked that room, which he had. He didn't want her to be afraid to leave her son with him. He might not know anything about raising kids, but he'd keep the boy safe and he could teach her a thing or two about not pandering to her son.

Angela joined them, and he turned over swing-pushing duties to her while he switched the car seat to the truck and grabbed a few more things she said they'd need. Then he pulled Grandma Shirley's Caddy into the barn and covered it.

Rest in peace, pink Cadillac.

He was surprised the thing had even made it this far, hauling all that weight. Maybe they'd work on the car a bit while Angela was gone. That would be another project to keep them busy until her return. Funny how all these projects were designed to keep him busy and not the boy.

Hatch didn't have a clue how to entertain a kid.

He stepped out of the barn and stopped. Laughter. He couldn't remember the last time he'd heard that sound around here.

She had her son in her lap, and they were swinging like a couple of kids. Hell, he would have thought she'd matured by now. Was she even twenty-one yet?

He had her birthday written down somewhere.

It occurred to him he kept harping on her age because he'd never felt that young or carefree. From very early on he'd been doing men's work alongside his father and grandfather. Then had come the day when he'd had a man's responsibilities.

No time for tire swings. No time for skinny-dipping or floating in an inner tube down the creek on a lazy summer afternoon. No time in the fall for football or making out under the bleachers after the game.

No time for tractor pulls. County fairs.

Or underage drinking down by the reservoir.

Okay, maybe *some* underage drinking.

Hatch didn't want to intrude on their fun, so he leaned back against the barn to watch. They didn't have a lot of time left together before she had to leave. He could give them a couple more minutes of playtime.

Now that he'd been medically retired at thirty, had a steady retirement income and all the time in the world to play, all he could think about was finding some meaningful work.

Was he crazy? Ranching was a hard life.

But also a rewarding one. And maybe he was looking to find some meaning to his.

He'd been at loose ends since finishing up around here. Of course, with the ranch he could always find another repair project if he wanted to. And he'd have plenty to keep him busy working a cattle operation.

Taking the house off the market, at least while he had custody of the boy, was the right thing to do. He'd decided that a couple days ago, when he'd heard they were coming. Even though he hadn't fully committed to any of it until today.

Angela caught sight of him and waved, then slowed the swing to a stop. He lifted a hand and pushed away from the barn. "You ready to go?"

She was flush with energy. Happiness.

"Mommy," Ryder said in a stage whisper that Hatch had no trouble hearing. "Is this our new house?"

"Do you want it to be?" Hatch asked.

The tyke nodded.

"Then consider it your new home."

Hell, he wasn't going anywhere anytime soon.

She eyed Hatch as if she didn't want him making those kinds of promises. Quite frankly, he didn't give a rip what she wanted. If she was going to dump her kid on him, then he was going to have some say in how the boy was raised. And he was going to give that kid the stability he'd been reared without.

Mommy's friend Hatch, my ass.

MADDIE HAD DINNER waiting for them when they returned to the boarding house. Afterward, it was time to get down to the legalities of the situation. Ryder was in another room coloring in front of the TV, and Maddie was doing her best to keep the kid out of the adult conversation.

Peaches had brought that folder with her, the contents of which were now spread on the dining room table. There were the papers he needed to sign and return. And the papers he needed to keep.

He picked up Ryder's birth certificate.

Father Unknown.

"You ever going to tell me the story behind this one?"

"It's none of your business." She snatched the document from him and put it in the keep pile she had going for him. Along with the kid's medical card and the log-in information to access his medical record online.

"I need the guy's name," he said, trying to be practical.

"I'm not giving you his name," she said. "I don't even know where he lives."

She dismissed the subject and moved on.

There were lists—plenty of them.

Ryder's routine. Favorite things. Favorite foods.

His birthday. And when he should be enrolled in preschool. Inoculations—the ones he'd had and the ones due.

Her contact information.

Step by step instructions for Skype.

Oh, she had plenty of demands, too. She wanted him to get connected. Purchase a cell phone with picture and video capabilities so he could send her photos. Lots of photos. And videos.

She wanted him to get a laptop. And an internet service provider. As if there weren't enough ways for them to stay connected, she'd printed out a "how to" for every social network out there.

And she was willing to pay for it all.

He didn't want her money. And he didn't want her help getting "connected." He'd had all the latest technology as a Navy SEAL. And while it had served a purpose at the time, he much preferred his low-tech existence now.

Then the real fight started. She'd given him limited power of attorney over medical decisions for her son and over her finances.

"Keep your damn money. How much can one kid eat?" he growled.

"I've already opened a joint bank account online in our names. Half my paycheck is going into it for Ryder's care. All I'm asking you to do is sign and return the signature card so you can access it. Kids cost money."

Six months into their marriage they should have been talking about divorce. Not commingling funds.

"And no guns. I'm serious, Hatch. Not anywhere near my child."

"I grew up around guns. I'm not going to suddenly forget everything I know about gun safety!"

His frustration at this point was cumulative.

They were going page by page though her parenting plan, and were getting down to the nitty-gritty.

Parenting temporarily was one thing. He didn't want the job permanently.

"Accidents happen," she said.

"Don't lecture me." He crossed his arms.

"I'm not trying to lecture you."

"No, you're trying to deflect from the real issue here with all this garbage." He picked up the fifty-some pages. "Which is that you don't really have a plan. I'm it. So you tell me what I'm supposed to do if you don't make it back!"

He about raised the roof with his raised voice. And there she was, struggling to remain calm in the face of his anger. "Just do the best you can," she said. "If you can't—" Her voice broke. "Just find him a good home. I've spoken with Will and Mia—"

"I want his father's name." Hatch kept his voice even.

"You are not sending my son to live with that man."

"Not if I don't have to."

"Not ever!"

Not only was she stubborn, she was also adamant. That set alarm bells off in his head. He'd assumed the sex with Ryder's father had been consensual. "You need to tell me what's going on here. Did he hurt you?"

She scoffed at his concern. "He was a prick, okay? But he didn't hurt me in the way you're thinking."

"Then he has a right to know he's a father."

"What makes you think I didn't tell him?"

"I know you."

"You don't know me, Hatch. You don't know me at all."

He knew that she was hot about something. He was getting a glimpse of that redhead temper in a way he never had. "I know you, darlin'," he said, trying not to lose his.

She shook her head. "I told him. As soon as I found out I was pregnant I told him. But just like you, he didn't want anything to do with me or my son," she accused.

"Where the hell is that coming from? What have I ever done except be there for you and your kid?"

"All right, you two," Maddie interrupted. "I've heard just about enough. Either kiss and make up or take the fight outside!"

"Mommy," the kid whined.

"Now look what you've done," Angela charged. What *he'd* done? Hatch took one glance at her comforting the kid, shot her parenting plan across the table at her and stormed from the room. There'd be no *comforting* the kid if she didn't make it home.

His aunt found him a half hour later, brooding out on the back porch with a beer in his hand. "Clayton, I've never been more ashamed of you in my life. You can't send that little gal off to war worried about her son."

He continued to stare out at nothing in particular. "I've never been more ashamed of myself." He tipped back his beer. He deserved the lecture that was coming his way.

"She can't see past your anger to the frustration, if anger is all you're showing her. You have to learn to let people in, Clay."

"Let 'em in where? I've got nothing in me."

"Oh, yes, you do," Maddie scolded. "You feel it. You just don't know how to recognize it. Or what to do with it. Would it kill you to admit you care what happens to her?"

He snorted at his aunt's simplification. He barely knew Angela Adams. But, of course he cared. He didn't want to see her hurt. Or dead. He felt responsible for her because he'd married her. Responsible now for her son. Except he didn't want to feel that way. He didn't want any of it.

From his perspective, the situation wasn't all that simple. He was angry, and justifiably so. And frustrated. Still, that didn't give him the right to bully her.

"You owe her an apology, at least."

He covered his embarrassment with a swig from the long-neck bottle. Finishing it made for a good excuse to hang out awhile longer. His aunt was right. He owed Angela an apology.

He wasn't angry with *her*. He was angry with himself because he should have seen this coming six months ago. And stopped her then. By sticking to his guns and saying no to her proposal.

ANGELA'S ROOM WAS the first to the left at the top of the stairs, and his was the first to the right. As he climbed the steps, he could hear her reading to her son.

Once he got to the landing he realized she wasn't the one reading. Not right then. She was explaining a recordable book to Ryder, letting him push the buttons, and they were listening together.

Hatch didn't want to disturb them, so he leaned against his bedroom door and eavesdropped.

"Mommy, I don't wanna stay with Hatch. He's mean."

"He's not mean, honey. He's got a soft spot right here."

Hatch didn't know what soft spot she was referring to, but her words produced a three-year-old's giggles. And made Hatch wish he was the least bit ticklish.

"Besides, he isn't mad at you. He's mad at Mommy."

"What'd you do?"

"It's everything I didn't do," she said somberly. "So you be a good boy while I'm gone and don't give him any trouble." More squeals sounded before mother and son settled down to reading again.

He could tell her his annoyance wasn't due to anything thing she did or didn't do. It was only him. Yet it *was* everything she did and didn't do that got on his nerves.

She was young and inexperienced. While he felt he'd been through it all a hundred times before.

He waited until their voices faded before he moved across the hall to her door. Folding his arms across his chest, he leaned his shoulder against the doorjamb. "Hey."

She offered him an uncertain smile. She looked tired, as if she couldn't keep her eyes open one second longer. Stretched out on the bed, pillows piled high and books all around, she stroked her son's hair.

Quite possibly, Hatch could be jealous of a three-year-old at this moment. "Can I put him to bed for you?" he volunteered, stepping into the room. Maddie had set the boy up next door, in a room with twin beds.

Angela glanced at her son. "No." She shook her head. "I want him with me." As if it were her last night on earth, and the boy was the only one she wanted to spend it with.

"I'll take good care of him," Hatch promised.

"I never had any doubt."

"WHAT ARE YOU DOING?" The next morning Hatch stood there covering himself with the floral shower curtain—his aunt's choice, not his.

"Going tinkle." Pajama bottoms around his ankles, the kid swung his feet back and forth from his perch.

"I can see that." Hatch grabbed a towel and wrapped it around his waist. "I meant what are you doing in my bathroom?"

Just as casually, he reached for his eye patch

and slipped it back on. Old SEAL habits died hard. Never let anything important get out of reach.

"Mommy locks the door."

"Ah, good to know for future reference. Hurry up and finish your business."

"I am hurrying up." But the little boy didn't appear to be in any hurry at all. "Hatch, is your tattoo the kind that washes off or stays on?"

"The kind that stays on."

"I have a tattoo." The kid lifted his shirt over his tummy. "It washes off," he said, then pulled his shirt back down.

"Sure enough," Hatch agreed, though he didn't recognize the faded and peeling character. And still the kid didn't go. "Is tinkle all you've got to do?"

"Uh-huh."

"Then why don't you stand up?"

The kid's blank stare gave him the answer. Because he was a little boy who'd been brought up by females. Hatch lifted the kid to his feet, raised the toilet seat and pointed. "Now try."

Hatch turned on the tap and listened.

Heard the tinkle. Heard the flush. Turned around as the kid hitched up his pajama bottoms. Then Ryder walked over to the wastebasket, dumped it upside down, and brought it to the

sink to use as a step stool. Hatch didn't say anything, just looked at the trash on the floor and
knew a moment of panic.

Kids were messy.

How was he going to handle that? He'd become
regimented in his own life, overcompensating for
the lack of discipline in his mother's. He liked
things neat and tidy.

On schedule and running on time.

Ryder climbed onto the upturned basket and
washed his hands, which he promptly shook off
and wiped on his pajamas. Hatch leaned over to
pass him a hand towel.

The boy watched him shave for a moment.
"What are you doing?"

"Getting rid of my whiskers. Hold out your
hand." Hatch pressed a little shaving gel into the
boy's palm. The boy smeared it on his face. Hatch
ran the comb through the gel. This was how his
grandpa Henry had taught him to shave.

Ryder carefully went through the same motions. "Hatch, how come you wear a patch?"

"I lost my eye." Hatch pulled back when the
kid reached up for a peek. "Hey," he scolded.

"Where did you lose it? Do you want me to
help you find it?"

Okay, wrong track. Try again.

"I hurt my eye."

"How did you hurt your eye, Hatch?"

"Are these questions going to go on forever?"

"Hatch, did you know that if you have a broken heart, you can eat a candy heart to fix it?"

"No, I didn't know that. Who told you that nonsense?"

"My mom." Ryder dug into his pajama pocket and extracted two candy hearts. One said Kiss Me and the other Hugs. From the other pocket he produced a gummy worm. "I don't have any eyeballs," he said sadly. "Do you want a gummy worm?"

"It's not my worm that needs fixing, kid."

"THERE YOU ARE." Angela had followed her son's voice into Hatch's bathroom. "Are you bothering Hatch?"

"Nooo," he said coyly.

"Yes, you are." She picked him up for a hug, then noticed the pile of trash on the floor and the upturned wastebasket. "Is that your mess? Go clean it up."

She patted her son on the butt to hurry him along.

"Sorry 'bout that," she murmured, averting her gaze from Hatch's bare torso. He wore nothing but a towel and a couple tattoos. She'd never seen them before. Hadn't even known he had ink down his arms. His broad shoulders and bare chest was the last image she needed to take with her to Afghanistan. She'd had a hard enough time falling asleep last night after everything left unsaid following their fight.

"Not a problem." He continued shaving. "I'll be done in a minute," he said, watching her watch him in the mirror. "Was there something else you needed?"

Shaking her head, she glanced down at her boots.

She was in uniform. Ready to go.

But in no hurry to leave.

"Come on, pumpkin, let's get you dressed," she said to Ryder. He jumped up into her arms.

"I'm not a pukin," he said.

"You're not?"

"Nooo."

"Are you a carrottop?"

"No, Mommy," he said seriously. "Can we go get some gummy eyeballs?"

"Not today, sweetheart."

HATCH PARKED THE TRUCK and hefted her seabag out of the back while she unbuckled her son from his car seat. Hatch didn't know why she'd insisted on dragging the kid to the Greyhound station. She was just postponing the inevitable.

But Ryder's chatter all the way to the bus depot made up for the lack of conversation between Peaches and him.

"Well…" He left the word hanging. The tension in the air felt as heavy as the seabag he dropped to the curb. "Looks like your bus over there."

A flight back to San Diego would have been faster, but he knew her aversion to planes. Plus a private with only six months in the service didn't make much money. A bus ticket was probably all she could afford.

As she crouched to say goodbye to her son for an entire year, he wondered if she now regretted her decision to join up. Good benefits, shitty pay and shittier duty. God, how he missed it.

Or was she feeling the surge of pride that came with putting on the uniform? Going off to do your duty. And knowing that every second of your life counted for something from here on out.

"You be a good boy now." She put on a brave front. "Mind Aunt Maddie and Hatch. You'll have so much to do on the ranch you won't have time to miss me. And I'll be back before you know it. Okay?"

For a little guy with so much to jabber about earlier, he sure didn't have much left to say. He just stood there nodding while his mother fussed over him.

"Can I get a big hug?" she asked.

The kid wrapped himself around her as though he'd never let go. Hatch hated to be the one to spoil the moment, but the driver was loading up the last of the bags now. He shot the man a curt nod in appreciation for the extra minute given them.

"Peaches…"

She glanced over her shoulder at the bus, its motor running. Put on her biggest smile yet. Planted a succession of quick kisses all over the boy's face, until he was squirming. Then pushed herself to her feet.

Anticipating a hissy-fit from the three-year-old, Hatch put a hand on the small shoulder to hold him back. But instead of encountering a fuss from the little boy, Hatch found a sticky hand grasping his.

Which left him with only one arm to hold her when Angela wrapped him in a hug. "Hatch," she said. "Take good care of him for me."

Looking into her eyes, he made that promise with a nod.

She squeezed all the air from his lungs with her shuddered breath as she whispered in his ear, "A year's a long time to a three-year-old. Please don't let him forget. No matter *what,* please don't let him forget me."

He felt that first tear trickle to his collar.

"Don't worry about a thing. We'll be fine."

Pulling away, she sniffed back her tears and put that brave smile on again. With a quick nod, she took a couple steps backward, then turned and hurried toward the bus.

The door closed and the air brakes released almost immediately. The driver was behind schedule, Hatch supposed. As the bus backed up, he wondered how military wives did it deployment after deployment.

Left standing on the curb, holding the little one's hand, he felt about as impotent as a man could, sending his wife off to war.

She'd worked her way to the rear of the bus and waved now.

Blew a kiss in their direction from that big back window. Hatch returned the kiss with a two-finger salute above his eye patch as she rolled out of sight.

"Hatch—" Ryder tugged on his hand "—how long is a year?"

Hatch hunkered down and roughed the little carrottop. He wasn't going to lie to the boy. "A year is a long time."

"That's what I thought." The little guy was working up to something with that trembling lip. But he didn't cry. He opened his little fist, which held two candy hearts.

"One for you and one for me?" Hatch asked.

The tyke nodded.

CHAPTER SIX

A year later (almost)

"So, CLAY, WHO DO WE have here?" The feed store owner winked and peered over the register. Hatch smoothed a hand over Ryder's hair. They'd been in the store a dozen times or more since Angela's son had come to live with him.

He'd be surprised if there was anyone left in town who didn't recognize this little carrottop.

"It's me, Mr. Grainger."

"No." Grainger continued to put on a show. "Ryder, is that really you? You must have grown two inches overnight."

"Today's my birthday. I'm this many." He held up four fingers.

"How many is that?" Hatch quizzed him.

"Four."

"Well, happy fourth birthday. I believe Mrs. Grainger said something about that." Mr. Grainger reached behind the counter and pulled out a wrapped present. "She wanted me to give this to you."

Ryder grabbed for the gift eagerly. Then looked to see if that was okay with Hatch. Ruffling the boy's head, he nodded. "What do you say?"

"Thank you, Mr. Grainger. You can come to my party if you want. And Mrs. Grainger if she wants. I don't have any more invitations because they were just for kids. But you can still come."

Once you got him talking he kept going and going.

"You're very welcome, young man. I'm afraid I can't make it to your party because I have to watch the store. But Cory and his grandma will be there."

Ryder scrunched his face in an effort to connect the dots between his preschool friend, Cory Grainger, and Cory's grandparents, Mr. and Mrs. Grainger, who ran the feed store. He was just becoming aware of the tangle of familial relationships.

Realizing Mrs. Grainger was both Mr. Grainger's wife and Cory's grandma was a big leap for him. A few months ago they'd implied Aunt Maddie was an honorary title. And here she was his very real great-aunt by marriage.

Grainger lifted the lid off the Dum Dum jar. "Can I offer your boy a sucker, Clay?"

Your boy. Hatch didn't know if he was just becoming more attuned to it because Ryder seemed to be searching for his connection to the world, but people referred to the boy as his more often than not these days, too. Ryder wasn't just Angela's son.

He was Hatch's stepson.

The first time someone verbalized that connections Hatch had had a hard time wrapping his brain around it. He hadn't thought of his responsibility to Ryder in quite those terms. Today he didn't even bat his good eye, but simply smiled and nodded.

"We're here about the ad in the paper," he said.

"Out back." Grainger led the way through the store, a mysterious and magical place with an array of odd merchandise. They passed through the birdseed aisle with its birdbaths and birdhouses, and a motion detector device As Seen on TV "that kept squirrels away from gardens and feeders."

Hatch used to love coming here as a kid.

Grainger didn't just sell feed for pets and livestock. Grainger's Feed & Pet Supply served as a centralized location for anyone wanting to off-load baby animals. The backyard was like a petting zoo.

Ryder ran toward the chicken wire pen where the whelps were tearing through the sides of a battered cardboard box in their eagerness to get out and explore. "Puppies!"

From the look of it, neither puppies nor the boy would be contained for very long. The six energetic pups competed for Ryder's attention with their yelping.

"What do you think?"

After offering to hold the wrapped present, Hatch unlatched the gate and unleashed the kid on the hounds. Or more accurately, blue heelers, a breed that got their color from a white coat with black hairs that gave the dog a bluish hue. The puppies all looked like little blue-gray rats with black ears. A couple had a black spot or two and one was completely gray.

"Would you like a puppy for your birthday?"

Ryder dropped to his knees amid the fray. "Hatch, this is the *bestest* fourth birthday present ever. All my life I've wanted a puppy."

Hatch got a good chuckle out of that one. He leaned over the fence and watched him roll around in the straw-filled pen.

Angela had planned ahead, leaving wrapped

birthday and holiday presents for her son. Hatch
had kept them hidden in the trunk of the Caddy.

He hadn't really thought about getting the kid
something until a couple of weeks ago, when
Maddie started making a fuss about party planning. She was back at the ranch right now, deco-
rating, while he and the boy had driven into town
for haircuts and anything else he could think of
to keep them out of his aunt's way for the next
couple hours.

Until he'd read the ad in the paper at the bar-
bershop, his big plan for the day had been a drive
to Walmart in Green River and let the boy pick
out his own present. This was definitely a better
plan.

Stew came running out the back after Alex,
barely able to keep up with his stepson. Hatch let
the boy inside the pen and Stew stopped to catch
his breath before sidling up next to them.

"When the hell did you get so out of shape?"
Hatch muttered. While Stew hadn't been a Navy
SEAL, he'd been in the Navy and had to maintain
a weight standard and physical fitness requirements.

"You have to ask?"

Stew had put on a good thirty pounds with his
wife's pregnancy. But Mia had lost her weight

after the birth of their daughter, Sophia, and Stew hadn't.

"Don't think I haven't noticed you've put on a few pounds," his friend added.

It was true. But only the twenty or so pounds Hatch had lost while in the desert heat. And afterward in the hospital. He raised his T-shirt a couple inches to show he still had abs of steel.

"I hate you," Stew said.

"Are you coming to my party?" Ryder was asking Alex.

"Yeah, we got you a present. I can't tell you what it is, though" Alex held out an action figure. "But I got one, too. Only yours is different."

"Alex!" Stew scolded. "You weren't supposed to tell."

"Hatch is getting me a puppy for my birthday." Ryder held on to two promising prospects, one a medium blue with black ears and a mask, with a patch just above his tailbone. The other also had black ears, and three big patches on his back.

"Dad, I want a puppy!" Alex turned to Stew in appeal. "Ryder gets one, so can I have one, too?"

"No," Stew said, "we just came here to look. Your mom would kill me." He turned back to Hatch. "Are you crazy? Have you even asked Ryder's mother?"

The boys had moved farther into the pen to chase down the pack. Although it looked more as if the pack was chasing them.

Hatch kept his voice low to keep little ears from overhearing. "Shouldn't I have done that?"

It wouldn't be his first blunder in child rearing. Angela wasn't always accessible when he had a question. Phone calls were reserved for true emergencies and there was no guarantee he'd even get ahold of her. The internet was their most reliable means of communication.

Though there could be lag time between their Q & A sessions. There were a hundred reasons for it, not all of them bad, but he found himself worrying when he didn't hear back from her right away. Whenever he couldn't reach her, however, he relied on Mia and sometimes Stew for guidance.

"Yeah," his pal said, beginning to sound like the voice of reason. "A puppy is a twelve- to fifteen-year commitment. You don't just bring one home on a whim."

Hatch and Angela had scheduled a Skype session for after the party.

"I guess I should put the boy off until I speak with her." He glanced over at Ryder. Down to one puppy. It looked as if he'd made his decision....

The pup with the black patch above his tailbone.

The boys were running in circles, squealing and inciting the pups to chase them.

"So which one are you going to get?" Stew asked.

"The one in the lead." The blue bundle of energy was nipping at, but not biting, Ryder's heels. He was also trying to keep the other pups in check. The alpha. "I've been needing a good herd dog. Picked up another two dozen head at auction the other day."

"Mia's been wanting a house with a yard," Stew said. "We get a yard, there's no excuse not to have a dog. Which one do you think I should get?"

"That pudgy little guy running at the back of the pack."

Stew took Hatch's good-natured ribbing in stride. "We could start running together in the morning. Maybe I'd lose some of this excess baggage."

"You could start with the ten miles out to my place every day. That ought to do it."

"Might not be that far." Will shoved his hands into his pockets and rocked back on his heels. "I'm thinking about buying the old Anderson place. If it's all right with you?"

Hatch was quiet for a moment. Fifteen years ago the Anderson property had been Henry land. One of ten 650 acre plots. Nine of which had been sold off. "Why wouldn't it be?"

Anderson was desperate to sell and Hatch had been holding out hope of getting it back until just now.

A pipe dream. He didn't have the kind of money it would take to piece Henry land back together. Not all of which was even available. Some of the land had been developed, and only four of the nine plots were on the market.

Anderson's land being the only one abutting his.

He looked Stew in the eye. "Of course it's all right with me."

And it was.

"Mia deserves better than a double-wide behind the shop, with my mother in the next room." Stew shuddered. "And right now the baby's in our room. The only other option is having Sophia and Alex share. That works for now, but it won't five years from now."

Hatch gave himself a mental kick in the pants for having teased Stew about his weight. His friend carried even more weight on his shoulders. Hatch had gone all through school and joined the

Navy with the Stewart boys, Will and his cousin, Big Al—Alex.

Big Al and Hatch had gone on to become Navy SEALS. Will never made it past the first qualifying round of physical fitness tests. After his first hitch in the Navy he'd decided military life wasn't for him, and he'd returned to the family business.

Meanwhile, Big Al, star quarterback, married his high school sweetheart and breezed through Basic Underwater Demolition/SEALs training. He'd been sitting to Hatch's left when the rocket propelled grenade ripped through their transport.

Shrapnel had taken out Hatch's eye, killed two of their team members and injured three others, including Calhoun, who'd lost his leg and two brothers.

Hatch admired Calhoun for a lot of reasons, not the least of which being the gunny was one tough son of a gun.

Alex Stewart had escaped without a scratch— not that Hatch begrudged him that. Except he was never the same again.

Survivor's guilt? Post-traumatic stress disorder?

Hatch didn't know what had made Alex Stewart take his own life. Only that he'd left his wife, Mia, devastated. Will Stewart, the most stand-up guy Hatch knew, had stepped in to pick up the pieces.

When his cousin's widow wouldn't eat, he'd fed her. When she couldn't sleep, he'd sat up with her all night. And when she couldn't get herself out of bed in the morning to care for her son, Will took care of Alex. When Mia had discovered she was pregnant with her dead husband's baby, and lost the child shortly after, Will had been there to cry with her.

A year after his cousin's death, Will convinced Mia to marry him. But somewhere along the way he'd convinced himself he wasn't good enough for his cousin's widow—the girl he'd had a crush on since high school. That she'd married him only because he was a convenient substitute.

That wasn't how Hatch saw it. Mia was the happiest he'd ever seen her. "It'll be nice to have you as a neighbor."

"You know I'm not a rancher, Hatch," Will said. "I just want the property for the house and the yard. A little hunting. And the damn dog I'm going to get an ass-chewing over." He glanced at the light blue runt his son held, and sighed. "If you ever want to expand, we could work something out regarding the land. You could buy it back or lease it."

"I appreciate it." Saying more than that would be like admitting he was ready to return to his own roots.

"WHAT DO YOU GALS DO for the Marines?" the guy across from Angela asked as they rumbled along in the back of the supply truck. "Aside from drive trucks?"

"You mean like this one you commandeered from us?" Maria Romano said in her tough New Jersey accent.

"We're mechanics." Angela never had gotten around to taking one of those powder puff car maintenance classes. Instead, she'd chosen automotive maintenance as her military occupational specialty. Mechanics often did double duty as drivers along supply routes, for the very practical reason that if a truck broke down there was someone on hand to fix it.

Provided they had everything they needed. Or could compromise enough to get the truck running again.

These guys weren't the enemy, but they didn't look like any of the Marines she knew. They had long hair. Overgrown beads. Wore a uniform of sorts. And looked as if they could move in and out of villages without attracting too much attention.

These men reminded her of Hatch when they'd first met.

The guy next to her wasn't talking, but he kept brushing his thigh against hers. Angela shifted in her seat and he bumped her again. It wasn't as if she'd never been in this situation before.

Bored men. Isolated duty.

Yeah, a few of them were bound to get out of hand.

"Son of a—" He let loose a howl. "What'd you do that for?"

"Sorry." She shifted the butt end of her M-16 from his boot. "Did I put my weapon down on your foot?"

He was tough. He could take it.

Intentional or not, she couldn't take any more of his cozying up to her. All she wanted was to get back to base in time to talk with her son on his birthday.

A guy sitting in the corner chuckled. "Better watch yourself, Shade. That's Hatch's wife you're messing with."

The hairs at the back of her neck stood on end. How did he know that?

They guy on her right straightened and put some space between them. And when she looked around, even the men who hadn't been bothering her were sitting up straighter.

The one in the corner moved out of the shadows, and she saw he was about her age. She'd never met him, but he seemed familiar.

Angela didn't know if these men were acting out of fear or respect. But whatever it was, she liked it. "Are you guys Navy SEALs?"

They hadn't volunteered any information when they'd stopped the supply caravan in the middle of nowhere. And turned the truck around after a brief chat with the officer in charge.

They were clearly men on a mission to return to base ASAP.

So the rest of the caravan had gone on, while she and Romano, the truck's duty drivers, had been ordered to stay with the vehicle and ride in back. Whoever was driving now was with these guys.

The guy across from her, the one who seemed to be in charge—at least back here—confirmed it with a nod. "I didn't know Hatch was married." He said it as if he didn't quite believe it. And why would he? It's not as if they'd sent out wedding invitations.

She touched the horseshoe nail with her thumb.

"How do you know Hatch?" she asked the young guy in the corner.

Should she have said "my husband" to drive home the point?

"Only by reputation," he said. "But some of these guys served with him. I'm sure he'd want to know if his old unit was disrespecting you. In any way," he added, for Shade's benefit.

They arrived back at camp a short while later.

Angela hopped down from the truck.

Maybe this had worked out better than she'd anticipated, since she was back long before her scheduled Skype time. Romano went to find their sergeant, to see if he'd even listen to their explanation, and to find out what he wanted them to do next.

There were troops in outposts counting on these supplies. But there was also safety in numbers, and Angela couldn't imagine the sergeant wanting them to set out on their own. But who knew when the next scheduled delivery was for that sector? They might need an armed escort.

She accepted the keys from the driver, who hurried off after the man who appeared to be their officer in charge. The rest of them seemed in no hurry to go anywhere. The young guy from the corner tailed her to the driver's door.

"So would you like to see a movie sometime, Angela Adams?" he asked.

"Are you hitting on me?"

"Maybe." His smile seemed sincere.

"As you pointed out—" she opened the door to climb in "—I'm married."

'I thought that was only a technicality."

She whipped around. "Who are you?"

She knew the Special Ops community was small and tight. But this guy's knowledge into her personal life was almost creepy.

"You don't recognize me, do you?"

She studied his handsome face. She'd seen that firm jaw and those green eyes before, but knew she'd never met him. His buzzed hair, sandy in color with blond highlights, could mean he was right out of boot camp, or that he just had a different haircut then the rest.

He carried the bag of a field medic, so if she had to guess, she'd say he was a corpsman. Did she know any hospital corpsman? Although that meant he was Navy, he might serve with Navy or Marine Corps units. "I give up," she said.

"We were recruited out of the same office back in Colorado. I went Navy. You went Marine. We ran into each other a couple times coming and going while I was on delayed entry. Keith Calhoun," he said, introducing himself. "My brother Bruce was your recruiter."

Huh, she didn't remember him at all. Probably because of everything she'd had on her mind back then. But now it all made sense.

"So you're a Navy SEAL?"

"No." He shook his head with a laugh. "Those guys just needed me for something." He sounded as vague as any Special Ops guy. "I'm fresh out of hospital corpsman school and Marine acclamation," he said of the mini boot camp the Marines put the Navy through because the two cultures were very different. "I'm here with you guys, the Marines."

They talked for the next half hour.

He was a year younger than her. He was smart, really smart. He had aspirations of becoming a doctor. And had enrolled in a Navy program that was paying his college tuition and would pay for med school. Of course, it required a commitment of several more years to the military. But he seemed to have it all figured out.

She wished she were that together.

"So will you have dinner with me?" He nodded toward the chow hall. "Best place around for dinner and a movie."

The only place. "If they don't need me anymore

today, I think I'm going to skip dinner and take a nap. Some other time maybe? Today's my son's birthday. We had a Skype chat scheduled for one in the morning our time, two-thirty in the afternoon his time."

After the party. She'd miss being there for the presents and the cake and candles. But this way he wouldn't miss out on his own party when Mom dropped in.

If she napped until midnight rations she would have just enough time to eat midrats and get to the computers for her scheduled chat.

"Tomorrow night, then?"

"Sure, why not?"

They set a time to meet up tomorrow that wouldn't interfere with her Skype schedule. She watched him walk away.

"Mmm-mmm-mmm," Maria said. "I bet he looks just as good coming as he does going."

"Shut up." Angela choked back a giggle. "You have such a potty mouth. He's just being friendly. He's from my hometown. His brother was my recruiter. And that's all there is to it."

"Sarge says we just have to return the truck to the motor pool and can call it a day."

"You, and you!" a mud-spattered Marine bellowed at them while climbing out of a Humvee. "You're coming with me."

"We have to return this truck," Romano said.

"You!" He pointed at a guy passing by. "Return this truck to the motor pool." He took the keys from Angela and tossed them over.

"Hey, I'm signed out for that—"

"I've already cleared it with your CO. I need two females in full gear, now. You two are in full gear." The back door of the Humvee opened from the inside. "You waiting for an invitation? Get in!"

Angela picked up her weapon, put on her helmet and moved toward the vehicle. Up close, she could see those weren't mud spatters covering his uniform.

They were dried blood spatters.

This was not going to be fun. Hoorah!

IT WAS AFTER TWO IN THE morning Wyoming time.

Ryder had fallen asleep on the couch around ten. Hatch had tried to sleep and couldn't. Being at the disposal of the military as she was, there were a million reasons why Angela might have missed their chat.

But twelve hours and no word on her son's birthday? As she'd once pointed out, Hatch was a worst-case-scenario thinker, and that fact was keeping him awake and pacing tonight.

He decided to check his email one last time and then call it a night. He'd been sending her hourly updates of his status in case she checked in online.

Hatch sat down at the desk in his den. Even though he preferred being outdoors, he still had books to keep for his small cattle operation, and had set up a nice home office.

Nothing from Angela, rescheduling. And Skype still showed her status as being off-line.

He was reluctant to shut the window down even now.

So he got out the scratch pad where he'd been doing his thinking. Stew had given him a lot to ponder today. Hatch's return to Two Forks Ranch was supposed to have been temporary. And now look at him. He was about as settled in at the ranch as a man could get.

After thirteen years of traveling the world, he knew there were still plenty of places he wanted to see, but he kind of liked this feeling of having roots.

And a home.

The question was did he want to risk the comfortable life he had now in order to expand? He'd been able to finance his small start-up operation out of pocket, and with only thirty-six head of cattle he wasn't near capacity for his own land, and was able to do it all himself.

He rubbed the bridge of his nose and under the edge of his eye patch. Getting up to pour himself another cup of coffee, he went into the kitchen and realized the pot was empty. He started another one and let the pup out while waiting.

Hatch stared out at the big, open night sky.

Smelled that crisp clean air. He could breath out here even with that unmistakable hint of cattle.

Buying or leasing land from Stew would allow him to expand the herd to two hundred. A relatively small operation and one that put him right back into the family business.

Still, he'd have to borrow or barter for the land and for cows, maybe a bull or two. He'd need to seed the pasture with alfalfa for hay in the winter, and supplement with feed when necessary. His income would be at the mercy of droughts and floods and whatever nature saw fit to throw at him. Not to mention the stock market.

He'd need a couple extra hands and the bank-roll to pay them. New equipment.

The list went on. He knew better than most

that too much debt in too short a time could turn a profitable operation south in a heartbeat.

When he went back inside and grabbed his cup of coffee, he was glad that he'd hesitated shutting down for the night. He heard that unmistakable sound of a video call ringing through.

He slid back into his desk chair and clicked to accept the call. Angela's face popped up on the screen. She had her hair pulled back and was sporting a deep tan. And that puke-colored T-shirt made her green eyes pop. "Hey."

"You're still up," she said, looking even more tired than he felt. It was the middle of the day in Afghanistan. He'd figured out a while back from a few sketchy details, and only because he'd been there himself a couple times, that she was at Camp Leatherneck, in the Helmand Province.

A big, six thousand U.S. Marine bull's-eye in the middle of the desert. Supporting ten thousand Marines on base and in outlying areas.

Sunlight streamed into the tent, and people moved in and out behind her.

"How was the party?" she asked.

"We had twelve screaming four-year-olds on a sugar high. Maddie says that's a good thing. Sorry you missed it."

"I'm sorry, too."

"What happened?"

"Don't ask."

Okay, he knew the rules. He'd had to play by them for years. That said, amusing anecdotes about coworkers were not off-limits. He still got a kick out of the fact that the girl with the pink Cadillac he'd found broken down on his ranch road had become an auto mechanic.

Good for her. "How's the motor pool?"

"As of today," she said, "I'm no longer part of that. I guess you'd call it a field transfer to MP. I don't know..." She looked down at her hands. She was wearing the ring he'd given her. "They haven't actually changed my MOS."

"What are you doing with the military police?"

"You know I can't tell you any more than that."

That wasn't good enough for him. MP didn't sound like a good fit for her. All the female MPs he knew were tough-as-nails Marines. And Angela thought she was tougher than she really was.

MP was one of those iffy jobs that wasn't considered infantry or closed to females. But in combat situations security was dangerous work.

He tried to imagine what she might be doing. Manning checkpoints? Search and seizure operation? Dealing with burka-wearing suicide bombers? Handling bomb-sniffing dogs?

The job was a lot more than the movie version of guys in white helmets harassing drunken sailors and Marines.

Working in the motor pool didn't keep her safe, but at least he knew what she was doing day in and day out. The conversation threatened to lull as he tried to push it into territory she couldn't discuss.

"How's Ryder?"

She'd changed the subject, her voice softening as it always did when she asked about her son.

"You want me to get him?"

"No," she exclaimed. Even though he knew she'd like nothing better. "Don't wake him. Was he terribly disappointed?"

"He's just over here on the couch. Fell asleep waiting for you. Let me get him."

Hatch was up and out of his seat before she could protest. "Ryder," he said, shaking the boy gently. "Your mom's online."

Disoriented, Ryder looked around. "Mommy?"

"On the screen."

Ryder ran to the computer, where he crawled up into the chair and knelt in front of the monitor. Folding his arms, Hatch leaned against the archway, close enough to assist and far enough to be out of the way.

"Hi, baby. I didn't mean to wake you up."

"Hatch let me wait up."

"Well, thank you for waiting. Did you have a nice birthday?"

He nodded. "Just a minute," he said, crawling down from the chair. He started to run away, then returned. "Be right back."

"Guess he has to go the bathroom," Hatch said, moving from the doorway to occupy the vacant seat. She appeared anxious as well as tired.

"He misses you," Hatch said.

She nodded. "I miss him, too."

Hatch's heartbeat kicked up a couple notches.

A few minutes into their conversation Ryder came running back into the room carrying Blue. "Look what Hatch got me for my birthday."

"A puppy?" Her onscreen gaze shifted from Ryder to him.

"His name is Blue," Ryder continued. "He's a boy."

Ryder stood next to the chair and held the pup with his distended puppy belly and other parts toward the screen. He went on and on about everything they'd learned today about Australian cattle dogs. And how much he love, love, loved Blue.

She kept her smile in place, but Hatch could see

by her eyes he was in some serious trouble here. "He looks like a real bundle of energy," she said.

"Oh, he is," Ryder agreed. He ran off again to put the puppy back in his pen in the kitchen.

"You bought him a dog without even asking me?" She kept one eye on Hatch and one eye out for Ryder's return. "What were you thinking?"

CHAPTER SEVEN

A FEW WEEKS LATER Hatch was standing in the Sweetwater County Airport with Ryder, knowing he was going to have to answer that question in person. The military had flown her from Afghanistan to LAX. The rest of the trip was on her time and her dime.

Hatch had offered to meet her at a larger municipal airport, Denver or even Jackson Hole, to try and save her a little bit of both. But she'd insisted on coming to them.

Knowing her parents had been killed in a plane crash, and that she'd chosen to fly rather than take some other form of transportation, told him how anxious she was to get here. To her son.

They were hanging out in baggage claim when he spotted her in her desert digital uniform, newer camouflage patterns created using modern pixels.

The Marines claimed a patent for the first design, but the rest of the services had borrowed the concept.

She'd dropped weight, to be expected in 120 degree heat, and from a distance looked like a little girl dressed up in her daddy's uniform. But up close no one would mistake her for a little girl anymore.

Nudging Ryder, Hatch pointed out Angela, thinking the boy would run to his mother. Instead, the four-year-old let the welcome home sign they'd made slip between their seats, and stared at her.

The eager anticipation of the past few days turned into a full-blown pout as he crossed his arms and turned away from his mother. Angela's approach was cautious. Hatch stood and they exchanged one of their trademark awkward hugs.

Then she knelt to Ryder's level. "Hi, honey. Mommy missed you."

The boy made a big show of keeping his back to her. Then he spun around and would have punched her if Hatch hadn't stopped him. "Hey."

He crouched down behind Ryder and turned the boy to face him. "We speak with our words. Not with our fists."

"It's okay." Angela instantly defended her son. "He's mad that I left him."

"It's not okay." Hatch stared her down, then her kid. "Do your feelings hurt?" Hatch asked, and the boy nodded. "Are you sad? And maybe a little confused? Your mom's changed. She even looks a little different, doesn't she?"

Ryder nodded again, and again.

"You look a little different to her, too." He had hold of the boy's arms and gave them a rub. "But you're happy she's home?"

He nodded with watery eyes this time. The boy wasn't the only one near tears. Angela was holding back her own.

"All those feelings add up to being angry only if you let them." Hatch was speaking from personal experience, but trying to put it into words a four-year-old would understand. "Are you ready to give your mom a hug and tell her you missed her?"

He nodded in encouragement and the boy turned and threw his arms around his mother.

WITH HER WELCOME HOME party still going on downstairs in Maddie's music room, conservatory—whatever it had been called in 1829—Angela had retreated upstairs. She wasn't sure how much more welcoming she could stand.

She and Hatch had started fighting on the drive to the ranch when he found out her plans included leaving the next day. Ryder was in the next room crying his eyes out because they couldn't take his new puppy with them.

This was turning into the homecoming from hell.

Not the homecoming she'd been dreaming about, anyway.

With jerky movements she folded another of Ryder's T-shirts and finished repacking his things into one suitcase. When they'd stopped by the ranch on the way here she'd grabbed without thinking. Now some of his things would have to go back into storage.

Or maybe she should just give them away. By the time they were settled anywhere he'd have outgrown them and they'd be into a different season.

He'd gotten so big in her absence she hardly recognized him as her baby boy. Judging by his tantrum in the airport, she appeared to be little more than a stranger to her own son. Even though they'd kissed and made up, it was Hatch's side Ryder stuck to as they were leaving the airport.

When they arrived at the ranch Ryder had taken her by the hand—after introducing her to Blue, of course—to show her the beautiful desert oasis they'd created for her out of Hatch's guest bedroom. She'd further disappointed them both by not spending even one night in that room.

She was on a tight schedule and had no time to prepare the boy for the changes that were coming his way. Hatch was in there now promising to take good care of Blue. If he had just asked her before promising her son a puppy, all this could have been avoided.

"And after he's housebroken," Hatch was saying, "he's going to need training in order to be a good cattle dog."

"I don't want to move to Missouri." Ryder's voice was thick with misery.

Angela didn't know if her presence would make things better or worse. So she stood in the doorway of her room to listen. The party downstairs was winding down. After she tucked Ryder in for the night she'd go back down and say goodnight to their guests.

If she angled herself just right she could see Hatch's broad back through the crack as he sat on the lower bunk and tried to reason with Ryder.

"It's only for a short time," he said. "Have you ever been to Missouri?"

"No."

"Then how do you know you won't like it?"

"Because I won't," Ryder said stubbornly. "And

I won't like Texas, either. And I won't like her new dog. How come Blue can't go to police dog school?"

"Because—" Hatch cleared his throat "—Blue is a cattle dog. He's not a police dog."

Angela crossed those few steps and knocked on the partially open door. "Can I come in?" She stepped in before anyone could make a fuss. Hatch, Ryder and Blue all turned to look at her. She could see in those puppy eyes that Blue blamed her, too.

"Can I get a kiss good-night?" She joined Ryder on the bottom bunk. "It's been a long time since I've had one of your kisses."

They smooched and she hugged him tight.

"Do you want me to read you a bedtime story?"

"I want Hatch to read." Ryder stroked Blue.

"Okay." So she was pushing it. She met Hatch's sympathetic gaze as she petted Blue with him. "Maybe Hatch will read us both a bedtime story. And maybe he'll even record a couple stories for us to take along?"

"Of course I will." Hatch picked up one of several books scattered at Ryder's feet. As if reading stories had become part of their bedtime routine.

"You're not coming with us, Hatch?"

"No," he said. "No, I'm not. Remember, I have to stay and look after Blue for you."

"And Aunt Maddie's not coming?"

"No, she has to stay and look after me." Hatch tried to make a joke of it, because he could see as well as Angela could where Ryder was going with this.

Her son went through the names of all his preschool friends and teachers, shopkeepers and ranchers, anyone in town he knew, as he began to realize he was leaving more than just his dog behind.

HATCH CLOSED THE DOOR with a quiet click and followed Angela into the hall. They had Ryder settled down now, and Hatch wanted to talk to her before she made a beeline back to her room

"Maybe you should think about letting him stay while you're in MP school," he suggested. "That's what, nine weeks? Another twelve for dog school?"

"He hardly knows me as it is."

"What's a few weeks?"

"In a few more months he won't even remember he has a mother."

"He hasn't forgotten you." He'd kept his promise to her. "He's a little confused right now, that's all. Frankly, so am I." Military schools were un-accompanied duty, meaning they didn't pay for families to tag along.

"It's no longer your concern. I promised you a divorce when I got back and you'll get it. Thank you for taking care of my son," she said in clipped tones.

But you're no longer needed. He could hear it in her voice.

"Where the hell is this coming from?" He backed her into her room. There was no good place to have this discussion, but the farther away from Ryder the better.

"What?" She stumbled backward and jerked away from him when he reached out to steady her. He didn't cross the threshold, just planted himself in the door.

"All that anger directed at me." He could feel his own temperature rising.

"I'm not angry."

"You're acting like it."

"Do you think this is easy for me? I know I'm making the selfish choice. Dragging him along for five months of extended stays in motel rooms. Just so we can spend evenings and weekends to-gether."

She turned away. Resting her arms on the dresser, she buried her head in her hands.

Hatch had done the math. She didn't make enough to cover the expense of five months even in cheap weekly-rate motels and on-base day care. She had the money because she'd been saving almost half her paycheck for an entire year. She had no bills except for their shared phone plan.

And he'd only tapped into their joint child care account for Ryder's preschool, but those two days a week of interaction with other kids wasn't much of an expense. And she hadn't spent much of the rest of her pay while in Afghanistan.

And wasn't that the real reason right there?

She'd just spent a whole year apart from her son.

"I could come with you," he suggested. "Help transition him."

She didn't turn around. "What good would that do?"

"Just a suggestion."

"You'd do that?"

The gratitude in her eyes when she turned toward him was worth any price. Even his freedom? Where was that thought coming from?

Maybe they shouldn't be talking divorce right

now. At least while she was in the service. He almost voiced the thought, but didn't.

"I appreciate the offer," she said. "But it's not necessary. And for what it's worth, I'm not mad at you. I'm jealous."

"Jealous?" The word and all its connotations took him aback. He'd heard from someone who saw fit to tell him his wife was hanging around with Keith Calhoun. Probably someone who thought Hatch should kick the young pup's ass. But he was cool with that. He wasn't jealous.

She should be seeing guys her own age.

What did *she* have to be jealous about?

"What's your first memory, Hatch? In it are you four, maybe five years old? A child's brain doesn't develop the capacity for long-term memory until well after thirty-six months. So unless I've traumatized my son—dropping him off here or taking away his first puppy—time spent with you is going to be one of his first memories. Yeah, I'm jealous."

CHAPTER EIGHT

SOMEONE KNOCKED AT HIS bedroom door. Hatch stayed seated and seriously thought about ignoring that knock. Chances were it wasn't his aunt. Or any of their guests who'd gone home hours ago.

Ryder didn't bother knocking. And Angela had no business knocking on his door after midnight.

Especially not when things were running hot and cold between them. One minute she was angry, the next apologetic. And the next jealous.

And really, it was all just adrenaline with nowhere to go. She'd been in a war zone for a year. While he'd been here watching her kid. If anyone had a right to be jealous it was him. He rubbed the bridge of his nose.

Damn headache. He couldn't even blame it on the booze. He hadn't had enough to get him drunk, let alone hungover.

He knew the drill. Angela probably just wanted to say goodbye. He'd never been any good at goodbye. He usually broke up with his girlfriends weeks before deployments.

To avoid those.

Besides which, what else was there left for them to say to each other?

Nice knowing you? Have a good life?

With a weary sigh he let the other shoe drop and padded across the carpet in his socks. Shirt unbuttoned, belt unbuckled, he was still decent. He had on a T-shirt beneath his dress shirt and his pants were still up around his waist.

But if she'd slipped into something sexy, well, all bets were off. He wasn't going to be responsible for what happened next. He opened the door to find Angela halfway across the hall to her room.

Looking very sexy in pajamas.

"Was there something you needed?" he asked. He kept his voice low. The house was dark and quiet, but Ryder was just down the hall.

Angela turned, and her smile seemed as uncertain as her stance. "Nothing." The huskiness didn't quite sound like her. "I just wanted to—"

Biting down on her bottom lip, she sought his approval with her eyes.

"Go back to bed," he said, none too kindly.

Her naked lips compressed to a fine line. "I just

wanted to say goodbye and thank you. You'll be filing for divorce once I'm gone?"

"That was our deal." He kept his expression benign.

"I guess we won't be seeing each other again. Until then, I mean."

"I'm sure our divorce can be handled through an attorney."

"I'm sure you're right. Thank you, again. For everything." She stepped in to kiss his cheek and he grabbed her, holding her back. His overreaction surprised them both, and they stared at each other.

"Did I hurt you?" he asked, still holding her at arm's length.

"No."

Not physically, maybe. But he *had* hurt her.

He could see it in her eyes.

"This is as far as we go," he said, relaxing his grip. But he didn't release her. And he honestly didn't remember later which one of them stepped in next. One minute he was staring into those soulful green eyes and the next his mouth was on hers.

Her kiss was soft. Sweet.

She gave away her whole heart in that kiss.

Gratitude.

There was a special place in hell for men like him. Who took what was offered without conscience. He tried to remember what it was like to be in his twenties. To fall in and out of love so easily.

She didn't love him. Even after all this time, she didn't know the first thing about him. She was grateful to him, that was all.

But he'd tasted that longing before. Saw it in her eyes as he pulled back. The desire to love and be loved.

That elusive promise of something more.

"Go!" He cleared the harshness from his voice. "You should go."

ANGELA KNEW HE WAS RIGHT. She should go. He'd given her plenty of opportunity.

But she'd come here for something. She couldn't remember what because she'd never been kissed like that before. "I don't want to," she murmured against his mouth.

Didn't want to go? Didn't want to save her kisses?

Didn't want to be sliding her arms around his neck and pulling his head back down for more.

She ran her fingers through his short hair.

He'd married her. Cared for Ryder. And asked

for nothing in return. She didn't have the words to tell him how much that meant to her.

And to be honest, she was more than a little curious since she'd married him. Had taken the image of him in nothing but a towel all the way to Afghanistan.

She didn't know the significance of his tattoos, just that she wanted to trace those sleeves of ink from his collarbone down both arms.

First with her fingertips, and then with her lips.

She pushed his dress shirt off his shoulders. Ripped at his T-shirt with impatience.

He stopped her wandering exploration and brought her mouth back to his. The stubble on his chin felt rough against her smooth skin.

Her cheek. Her neck. And lower.

Her heart raced as he traced the strap of her pj's and branded her shoulder. His hands slid up her waist to her ribcage, taking her top along with them.

He stopped his trail of kisses long enough to lift the tank top over her head. His good eye glazed over as he tossed the top aside and looked down at her breasts with pure masculine appreciation. And then they were chest to chest, kissing again.

She felt the cool metal of her dog tags.

And the tickle of hair on his chest. Not enough to hide the definition. But enough to tease her fingertips as she reached for his waistband.

He moved her backward toward the bed.

The only boy she'd been with had been her age at the time, seventeen, with an underdeveloped and hairless chest. The only other thing she remembered about that night was how drunk they'd both been. And how much he'd hurt her both during sex and weeks afterward when she'd told him she was pregnant.

Thank God she wasn't that young and stupid anymore. She'd turned twenty-two in May, the week before Ryder's birthday.

But Hatch liked to draw attention to their age difference. He'd turned thirty-two in April. So she teased him about it now as she curled her palm around his erection. "Show me what you've got, old man," she whispered in his ear.

Thirty-two wasn't old. Thirty-two was, oh, my God, experienced. And not shy about standing over her while taking off his pants. Thirty-two didn't rush her as his knee hit the mattress by her hip. He scooted her up toward the pillow and slipped her pajama pants off at the same time.

Thirty-two was all smooth moves.

She didn't tense up until she felt his other knee

between her thighs. Holding himself over her, he reached into the nightstand for a condom.

"I'm on the Pill," she volunteered. She had been since shortly after Ryder was born.

"That's good to know, but a naive thing to say. You should always insist the guy wear a condom."

"More dating advice?" she teased. What a strange thing for a man to say to his wife, as they were about to make love for the first time. But he set the condom aside. "What happened to wearing a condom?"

"A husband should have some privileges." His voice was a husky rasp of desire.

Propping himself up on his elbow, he took his duties as a husband very seriously. There wasn't an inch of her body that he didn't explore. Or an inch of his body that she didn't come to know intimately. By the time he entered her, she was more than ready for him.

She bit down on his shoulder so as not to embarrass herself with screaming. She'd never experienced anything like it before, let alone felt the need to tell the world about it.

All she wanted at this moment was to lie here and languish in the afterglow.

Stretched out on top of him, Angela watched as he kept trying to drift off to sleep. She knew she should let him. But she wasn't ready to take that walk of shame back to her room.

Where she'd realize allowing herself to feel anything at all for the man she'd married was a mistake. Big mistake. Since their marriage agreement included a preordained divorce. She stroked the scar on his brow, memorizing all the lines of his face.

He lifted his hand, but didn't try all that hard to stop her when she pushed that black leather patch off his handsome face. "If I have to be naked, you should be, too," she told him.

"I'm not going to argue with a woman who has her knee pressed up against my groin."

She compared his good eye to the other.

This close she could tell the one was made of glass. For one thing, the pupil didn't dilate and his real eye had adjusted for the dim lighting. And reflected his desire.

"Am I looking at you funny?" he finally asked, when she didn't look away.

"I don't know. Are you?" She laid her head on his chest and listened to his heartbeat. Hard to believe she'd come here just to talk and now she was lying naked on top of him. Harder to believe that she could feel this satisfied and still want more. Want him.

He stroked her thighs. Her bottom. Her neck.

Leaving delicious trails of longing.

She wanted him again so much it hurt.

Her own heart skipped a few beats as she acknowledged that it wasn't just his body she wanted. She wanted this connection. This feeling.

She wanted it to be real. Even though she feared it wasn't.

She was leaving tomorrow. "Will you miss me?"

When he didn't answer, she lifted her head and propped her chin with her hands flat against his chest, prepared to wait him out. Because she wanted to hear him say he wanted her, too. She knew he wanted her, too.

He took his time stroking her hair. "What is it you want?"

"Hatch." Her breath caught on his name.

He pressed his fingers to her swollen lips. "Shh, besides that," he murmured. "I know that's what you think you feel. But it's not." He spoke with the same tenderness he'd spoken with all night, but his words left her cold. "I made you feel good. You made me feel good. Let's leave it at that."

His hand at the small of her back felt warm against her cooling skin. Warmer when he cupped her bottom. And downright hot when he dipped between her legs.

Heaven help her, she wanted him to keep on touching her like that. Which just proved his point. That he could make her body feel good.

Oh, so good. She moaned from somewhere deep inside. And without hearing the words she longed to hear.

He was right. She was being naive.

Nobody fell in love after one night of passion.

And damn him, didn't he make her come again, and this time with just the talents he had at his fingertips.

She bit her bottom lip. *Do not cry in front of him.* All this sex had been her idea to begin with. But she wanted to burst from everything she was holding inside. She had nowhere to go with what she was feeling.

His hand slid up her spine to her nape.

He pulled her head down for a kiss and rolled over on top of her. "All you have to do is ask."

"I don't know what it is I want."

"Yes, you do." He stared down at her. "And just so we're both clear, you didn't have to sleep with me to get it. Why don't we put off the divorce indefinitely? At least until you're out of the service."

"I need you." She reached up to touch the scar

that cut through his eyebrow. He probably hated that. And the way his lid drooped more than the other. She thought it looked sexy.

She reached up and kissed him then. But this time was different. This time he took without giving back.

She wished she could say she didn't come as he pumped into her. But he was right. There was love and then there was lust. He found his release and she rode it all the way to the end.

"JUST STOPPED BY to see how you were doing," Stew said as he entered the big equipment barn. His voice echoed in the mostly empty steel structure. "Haven't seen much of you lately."

Hatch rolled out from underneath the Caddy and wiped the oil stains from his hands.

Maddie had given Angela her old Honda CRV to drive to Fort Leonard Wood, Missouri, eight weeks ago. The Marines did their military police training with the army. And their dog handler training at Lackland Air Force base in San Antonio, Texas.

"Doing all right." He sat up and scrubbed Blue behind the collar. Content just to be near him, the puppy settled back on his haunches and then lay down.

Hatch made sure the dog got a good workout in their twice-daily training sessions. But by far the pup's favorite pastime was chore time, when he followed Hatch out into the field to check on the herd.

Ryder would be disappointed to learn these loyal breeds tended to have only one master.

"Quiet around here," Stew commented.

He meant without the boys running around.

"About time I had some peace and quiet." Hatch tossed the rag aside and pushed himself to his feet.

"Have you heard from her?"

Not as often as he'd like. He didn't like to dwell on her leaving. She may have been his for a night, but she'd never been his to keep. "They're doing fine."

"Did she ever say why the switch to MP? I mean, nobody gets guaranteed dog handler school."

"She's part of a new program to train an all-Afghani-female militia. From what I understand she was pulled into it, not voluntarily. The Marines were training a local group when Afghani women started showing up demanding to be armed and trained. The Marines sent them away."

Hatch closed the hood of the Cadillac and

leaned against the car. "The insurgents found out about this group of women. Kidnapped the eight-year-old son of one of them and killed him. The next day double the number of women showed up demanding to be trained, including the mother carrying her dead son."

Stew shifted uncomfortably. "I can't imagine."

"The MPs on duty didn't know what the hell to do, either. They sent someone back to base to grab the first two available female Marines, which happened to be Angela and another mechanic."

Hard to believe he was talking about the same scared girl with the broken-down Caddy.

"Anyway, I guess they liked the way she handled herself, and offered her the chance to be part of this military training of Afghani females."

Pride and fear waged within him whenever Hatch thought about her in this new position.

"So did you get all settled in at the new place?" he asked. He had helped the Stewarts move into their new home the weekend after Angela and Ryder left.

"I'm not tripping over boxes anymore, if that's what you mean."

"Good. Because I've been to the bank and there's something I'd like to talk to you about."

CHAPTER NINE

Five years later

ANGELA FIDDLED WITH HER wedding band during takeoff. Because of her uniform she'd been upgraded to first class for this commercial flight from Kuwait to California.

The man beside her, a suit-and-tie businessmen, had offered her his window seat, which she'd declined. She white-knuckled the armrests as the aircraft roared down the runway, picking up speed.

There was that moment of weightlessness before the jet started to climb and she started to relax—although she wouldn't feel totally relaxed until after that first drink. Not that she was a drinker.

Or needed a drink to relax.

It's just that she'd already done the whole take-off and landing thing once today, when she'd flown in from Afghanistan on a military C-130 Hercules. And she still hated flying with a passion.

Plus she hadn't had any R & R in six months. One drink would probably put her to sleep.

The flight attendant came around with complimentary champagne. Angela eased her death grip on the armrest to accept a flute. "And could I get a chaser? A shot of Jack?"

"Make mine on the rocks. And we'll have two of those." Her seatmate offered a reassuring smile and went back to reading *Fortune* magazine.

"Uh-oh," he said a short while later. "The ring comes off."

"Excuse me?" She tucked the horseshoe nail into the breast pocket of her desert cammies.

"Sorry," he said, raising his glass. "I've been watching you wrestle with that decision for the past half hour. Deployment must be hard on a marriage—"

"Oh, no." She glanced at the tan line the ring had left. She always took the silly thing off on the flight home. Always. "I'm not married. Well, technically, I guess I am."

"Separated?"

And didn't he have a devilishly handsome smile?

She was used to men with shaved heads and

flak jackets, barking orders at her all day. She wasn't used to men with three-hundred-dollar haircuts and six-thousand-dollar suits—looking as though they'd stepped off the cover of *GQ*—willing to listen. "It's a long story."

"It's a long flight."

"LOOK AT THE SIZE of that rock!" Maddie pulled Angela inside the boarding house, and a short while later they were seated at the kitchen table. "So where'd you meet him? And when do we get to?"

"On the flight home from Kuwait." Her third tour in six years, and second time in Afghanistan since she'd been chosen as one of a handful of women selected to train an all-female militia. "I'm not sure when. It's complicated."

"By complicated you mean Clay." Maddie raised an eyebrow above the brim of her teacup.

Angela stirred honey into her cup. "The wedding is in six weeks, Maddie. I need to be divorced by then."

"Quite the whirlwind romance."

Six weeks. She could practically hear Maddie doing the math in her head. She'd met Jake just six weeks ago. And in six short weeks she'd be Mrs. Jacob "Jake" Jeager.

"It's as much of a shock to me as it is to anyone." She set the spoon aside. "He loves me, Maddie. And I love him." She'd been with three men in her life. Only one of them had ever said *I love you. I want to spend the rest of my life with you. Marry me.*

Didn't she deserve that?

"Then, what's the problem?" Maddie prodded gently. "You *have* mentioned that you're married? And that you have a son?"

"Of course. I told Jake everything about my life in the first sixteen hours and forty-five minutes after we met." The time required to get from Kuwait to LAX. She took a deep breath. "Except I may have skipped one very fine point... I didn't think it any of his business at the time, but then we got engaged and he suggested an annulment—"

"Clay would never go for *that*."

"Wouldn't he?" Angela said with a touch too much sarcasm. She wasn't so sure. He'd probably like nothing better than to retract the past six years. "I'm not asking him to," Angela said for clarification. "But I am going to file for a divorce."

"Oh, Angela. Of course I'm happy for you." The woman was all sympathy. But not for her.

"It's just that you and Clay have shared custody for so long…"

Because she'd spent three of the past six years deployed. "Even if I wasn't getting married, I'd still be leaving the service and moving on. It's time, Maddie."

"I know," the woman said with tears in her eyes. This divorce would be messier than Angela had ever imagined. "Please don't say anything to Hatch until I've had a chance to talk to him."

"TIME TO PUT AWAY THE GUNS." Hatch pocketed his cell phone. "Aunt Maddie just called. Your mom will be here any minute."

Blue yapped twice and took off down the road.

"What?" Ryder poked his head around a cutout of Bad Guy and shot off another round of neon-colored paintballs. Hatch caught a pink one in the shoulder and dived behind a hay bale to fire back. Their game continued for another ten minutes until Ryder broke cover.

Hatch took aim, fired—and plastered the SUV coming around the bend with the blue heeler chasing the rear tire. Angela slammed on her brakes.

Hatch pushed back his visor. "Ah, shit!"

"Busted." Ryder removed his helmet. "For the

record, Hatch, this is the coolest ninth birthday present ever. Even if we're both grounded for life."

"Where do you think you're going?"

"You hit her hybrid. She's gonna be pissed."

Hatch hauled him back by his coveralls. "She'll be so happy to see you she won't care."

Angela got out of the car in question, gaping at the neon-green spatters on her windshield. "You hit my car!"

She stood in the middle of the road in her blue jeans, car door thrown wide and hands raised in disbelief. Now, wasn't that a familiar sight. And damn if she still didn't take his breath away whenever he saw her.

Which hadn't been often.

But often enough to make him ache for something just out of reach. He'd decided a long time ago to keep their relationship in the friendship zone. But that didn't mean he couldn't remember how it had been between them.

Blue sat on his haunches at Angela's feet, waiting to get noticed. Hatch liked blue heelers for their smarts, but this one could sometimes get himself into trouble.

Although this time Hatch looked like the only one in trouble. Angela bent to scratch behind the

Australian cattle dog's ear, until one hind leg twitched in pure ecstasy.

Lucky dog.

"You hit my car," she repeated as Hatch got closer.

"Wasn't aiming to." He removed his helmet and finger-combed his hair. "Of course, my aim ain't what it used to be."

She rose to her feet. "That's always been your excuse."

"How many times have I used it on you?"

"For a paintball spatter, not once."

"Good, 'cause there's only one other time I recall trying to chase you off my property. And look where that got me." He leaned in for that awkward hug he knew was coming. You'd think they'd have figured it out by now.

"Look at it this way, Mom," Ryder said. "At least it's the same slime-green color."

"Come here, you." She laid her cheek on top of her son's paint-speckled head. "I won't be able to do this much longer. You've grown another couple inches since I last saw you."

Hatch gave mother and son their space. He wiped down her windshield and picked up her seabag from the back. He let Char, short for Charlie, out of her crate. The bomb-sniffing dog went immediately to her handler's side and exchanged a cautious sniff with the other dog.

Angela had been gone less than a year this time, six months overseas. And another six weeks back in the States before she could get away from her post.

Normally, Ryder lived in an off-base apartment with his mother when she was stateside, since the waiting list for base housing was so long. And Hatch could have brought the boy to her. He'd done it once already. But she'd said something about having to stay in the enlisted barracks until she had their living arrangements all figured out.

So they'd agreed it was in the boy's best interest to finish out the school year here in Wyoming.

The kid started to squirm before she let go.

"Sorry I missed being here for your birthday," she said to him.

Ryder shrugged. "No biggie."

"It *is* a big deal. But it won't happen again, I promise." She squeezed him to her side and they started walking arm in arm toward the house. "How do you like the Nintendo DS I sent you?"

"It's cool."

"Not as cool as a paint gun, though, huh?"

Hatch heard that twinge of jealousy in her voice as he fell in step beside them. For some reason she always thought Ryder preferred his presents to hers. But if she could just see the way the kid tore into any package from overseas, she'd realize how wrong she was.

Never missing another birthday was not the kind of promise a Marine could make. There were other hints—the housing excuse, for one—that she might be thinking about getting out of the service.

Hatch knew the closer she'd reached the end of her six-year enlistment, the more she wrestled with the decision, because they'd discussed it. A lot. But that deadline had passed while she was in Afghanistan, and he hadn't heard a thing about her final decision.

Which might have been what she couldn't spit out over the phone during their last conversation. Near as he could tell she was once again homeless and jobless, like the day she'd been desperate enough to ask a total a-hole to marry her.

They'd done a lot of talking over the phone and through email these past six years. But not once had they ever spent more than three nights under the same roof.

So how was he supposed to have convinced her to stick around for a while?

ANGELA STOOD at the kitchen sink, wiping down her paint-smeared T-shirt with a wet paper towel. She'd taken off her engagement ring when she'd stopped to open the cattle gate. The no trespassing sign still had the bullet hole from the day Hatch had tried to scare her off.

Well, he hadn't, and here she was about to hand him that divorce she'd promised him all those years ago. This should be easier than it was. It was what they both wanted.

Their marriage had served a single purpose. And they'd only stayed married as long as they had because of Ryder.

She'd offered to file for divorce after that first deployment. Nearly dropped to her knees with gratitude when Hatch had suggested they keep things the way they were for as long as she was in the service. Well, she no longer was. And was not only going to miss the Marine Corps, but was also going to miss Hatch.

He'd made it so easy for her. He and Ryder had bonded from the start. And he was always there when they needed him. But she didn't need him anymore.

That sounded so selfish. She took another swipe at her shirt. That was not how she meant it at all. She just meant they didn't need to impose on him any further.

He wasn't her husband in any sense of the word. Wasn't even Ryder's real father, though at times she wished he were.

And, yes, at times she'd thought about the sex. Wanted the sex. Even times when it would have been convenient to have sex with her predestined ex.

But she didn't need to be screwing around with the relationship when what they had—rather, didn't have—worked for both of them. And her son.

That, and because like most headed-for-divorce couples, they couldn't spend more than a few days under the same roof without fighting. So by some unspoken agreement she just made sure she never stayed that long.

"I don't think the stain'll come out that way." Hatch stepped into the kitchen. "Your bag is in your room."

"Thanks." She tossed the paper towel into the trash and held the wet mess she'd made of her T-shirt away from her body.

"The paint's not indelible." He dampened a dishcloth and wrung it out for her. "Face."

She put a hand to her cheek and came away with green paint on her fingertips.

"Just a little." He smiled. In fact, he smiled a lot more these days.

"Maybe I'll just go up and take a shower."

"Ryder is using the bathroom in the hall. You're welcome to use the shower in mine."

Obviously, he'd already taken a quick one—his hair was still damp. She liked the way he wore it these days. Not too long. And not too short.

"The place looks great, by the way. I'm surprised you have any time to play. Did I see more of those red cows out in the pasture?"

"Red cows?" he teased.

"Red Angus," she corrected. He'd told her a dozen times. Angus beef. She bought it in the grocery store. But even knowing where it came from hadn't turned her into a vegan yet. "How big is the herd now?"

"About as big as it can get without expanding even further." He could probably give her a number off the top of his head. But according to him, asking *that* question was like asking a rancher how much money he had in the bank. A cattleman could *volunteer* the information. Discuss it with his buddies. Even brag about it. But for her to ask was rude.

She knew he'd doubled the size of his ranch by buying up some neighboring properties that had once been in his family. He had to feel good about that. And he'd hired help.

"We make time," he said.

"Time for what?"

"Playing."

Oh, yes, playing. That's what they'd been talking about. She used the damp cloth on her flushed cheeks. He hadn't even meant the word suggestively.

Ryder bounded down the stairs. "Have you asked her yet?"

"Let your mom get settled in."

"Asked me what?" She looked from her son's excited expression to Hatch's poker face.

"How long you were planning on staying," he said.

"Just until school's out." The requisite three days. Wednesday, Thursday and Friday. Because by Saturday the two of them would be fighting about who knew what.

Best to go in, get out. Grab her son.

And no one got hurt.

"That's only until the end of the week," Ryder whined. "Not even a week. Not even a half a week."

"It's half a week," she argued.

"He'd like to stay through the Fourth of July."

"For the county fair—"

"Ryder, that's a whole month!" Being caught off guard added an edge to her voice, which she attempted to tamp down. "We can't stay that long for a fireworks display. We have a lot of fun things planned for this summer."

A wedding. Moving. Yeah, she couldn't think of one fun thing in store for a nine-year-old boy.

Nine? Where had the time gone?

Angela made a mental note to squeeze in something fun this summer. "What if we compromise and stay an extra week. We could go to a Rockies game and Elitch's."

She used his favorite sport and the amusement park to try to bribe him.

"That's not staying. That's driving all the way to Denver. Just 'cause you don't like it here doesn't mean I don't like it here."

"I like it here." She'd traveled the world and this ranch was the only place that… Yeah, he was right.

The house was comfy and cozy and all that. But she'd always had that restlessness about her. Something she felt even more acutely while she

was here. Which wasn't all that often, thank
goodness.

But often enough to make her feel she didn't
belong. The ranch was home. Just not her home.

Ryder had always felt differently, and for good
reason. How attached he'd become was scary. To
the state of Wyoming. The ranch. Hatch.

"I'm sorry, son," she reiterated. "We just can't
stay that long."

The Marine Corps had been the perfect fit for
her. Travel, good benefits and job security. Except
those year-long deployments took her too far from
Ryder. And for too long.

So she had put all her effort this year into finding a more perfect compromise. And then she'd
found Jake, and didn't have to look any further.

Because it was all so perfect.

When they'd landed at LAX, after what should
have seemed like an interminable flight, he'd
asked her to dinner. By the end of the evening
he'd offered her a job.

She'd already been job hunting online for
several months. Not shopping around for a new
husband. At twenty-seven she was a strong, independent young woman.

Career-minded. Not man-crazy.

The option to work within his company, Black-

Watch, was not off the table just because she was marrying the CEO. In fact, Jake had a love-hate relationship with the high-tech private security firm his father had started from the ground up.

Coming from military Special Ops, he had a different vision for the company. And she looked forward to being his partner in all things.

"But what about cattle dog trials?" Ryder argued. "Hatch said I could enter Blue this year."

"What's a cattle dog trial?" Some days she and her son spoke two entirely different languages. Thanks to Hatch.

"Dog competition," Hatch clarified, for the most part staying out of their discussion.

"What kind of competition?"

"For junior handlers," Hatch said.

"Hatch promised last year I could enter Blue this year. I've been working really hard."

"I'm your mother. I have veto power over Hatch." She met his single-eyed gaze over Ryder's head. "We're staying to the end of the week. And maybe next week. But that's it."

"You missed my birthday. You make me miss everything! I hate it when you come home!"

CHAPTER TEN

LATER THAT EVENING Hatch joined her out on the rear porch. "I recognize that thousand-yard stare."

Angela went back to crimping her wet hair with a towel as she gazed into the stormy sky. Lightning flashed in the distance. "It reminds me of tracer fire."

Thunder rumbled and she tensed.

"You'll get used to it." He twisted the tops off two bottles, tossed the caps into a bucket by the door and offered her a beer.

She let the towel drop to her shoulder and reached for the bottle.

He pulled it away. "You twenty-one yet?"

"Are you kidding?" She wrenched it out of his hand. "At the moment I feel much older than twenty-seven."

"He didn't mean it," Hatch said, bringing his bottle to his lips. "You know how he gets."

"I know." She eyed the beer in her hand as if she could forget, and took another sip.

"Remember your first deployment?"

Ryder hadn't recognized her when she'd returned from Afghanistan following that first tour of duty. When he'd realized she was his mother, the same mother who'd left him for a year, he got mad. Balled his little four-year-old hands and would have hit her, right in the airport, if Hatch hadn't intervened.

Every time since there'd been a fight both coming and going. Pre- and post-deployment parenting classes helped her to at least identify the problem. Pre-deployment was the "I'm going to hate you now so I don't miss you when you're gone" stage.

The phenomenon happened between spouses, too.

Similar to what Hatch called nature's fight-or-flight response, psychologists called it the fight before the flight.

Coming home, there was always that readjustment period where Ryder tested her, and she was the bad guy while Hatch got to be the good guy.

Post-deployment was the "why did you leave me if you love me?" stage.

Or the "prove to me that you love me now that you're home."

The fight after the flight.

Which made it seem that a lot of fighting went on in military families. Not necessarily. Just a lot of opportunity to become stronger and closer as a family.

It was all about how you weathered those storms.

"Was I too quick to say no?"

"In a perfect world I would have had time to talk you into it."

"You think so?" She turned to sit on the porch rail, dangling the beer bottle from her fingertips. "And just how would you have done that?"

"Well," he said, putting his boot up on the lower rail right next to her bare foot. "There is the guilt trip. To begin with, you did miss his birthday."

"Working good so far."

"The rest isn't pretty," Hatch said. "There's begging, pleading and crying on my part. And I'm fairly certain I put him off last year by promising him this year." He sounded sheepish. "This is the last year he's qualified to enter in that division. The older he gets the stiffer the competition."

"You promised my son he could enter cattle dog trials?" Kind of hard to keep the accusation out of her voice when the guilt trip was working. "And now I have to be the bad guy. Gee, thanks."

"The sport's harmless enough."

"I don't know, Hatch. The Fourth of July—"

"Isn't that far off. You must have some leave on the books." He continued to try to coax her into it.

She had so much to tell him she didn't know where to begin. "I cashed out."

In militaryspeak, she meant she'd sold back the leave she'd carried on the books at the end of her enlistment. Of course, she and Hatch did occasionally speak the same language.

He dropped his boot to the porch and straightened.

"You can't be that surprised. It's all I've talked about for the past year."

"Guess I hadn't realized you'd reached a decision." He slid a hand into his front pocket and took another swallow of beer.

She glanced down at the bottle in her hand before looking him in the eye again. "It's why I was stuck in San Diego so long after returning from Afghanistan." Her enlistment had ended before her deployment, so she'd signed a voluntary extension to complete her assignment. "I had to process out of the Marine Corps—"

That and the adoption process for Char had taken a while.

"You could have told me all this over the phone. It's not like we didn't talk at least once a week."

Sometimes more.

Or less, since she'd met Jake.

"Everything was still up in the air after I landed. My six years were up. It was leave now or sign on for another six-year hitch. You know the drill," she said, struggling not to get too irritated with him.

Because, heaven help her for admitting this, he was right. He spent just as much time with her son as she did. The very least she could do was keep him informed. "I really didn't know what I was going to do until I had a job offer to fall back on."

"You have a job?"

Now who was getting downright surly? It wasn't that she'd meant to keep him in the dark. Just that it all happened so fast.

Jake. The job. The engagement.

There would never be a good time to tell him.

So tell him now.

"Yes, I have a job—"

"Mommy." Ryder stood in the doorway, sounding more like the little boy he'd once been than the nine-year-old he'd become. He'd long ago given up calling her Mommy to call her Mom.

Once again she wondered where the time had gone?

"Thunder keeping you awake?" She pulled him to her side. She knew better than that. He was just like her. He liked falling asleep to the sound of a storm.

He shook his head. "I just wanted to say I'm sorry. I really am glad you're back."

"I'm sorry, too," she said, giving him a squeeze. "Let's get you back to bed."

Ryder was old enough and independent enough that he didn't need the smothering. But suddenly any excuse seemed like a good excuse for disrupting her conversation with Hatch. Even tucking her nine-year-old back in bed.

She put a hand on his shoulder to follow him back inside.

"Angela." Hatch brushed her arm.

He rarely touched her, so that in itself was a surprise. But to feel the voltage his touch generated…

She looked from her arm to his face.

"Don't go."

HATCH FINISHED HIS BEER out on the porch alone. That was some bullet proofvest she wore. His words hadn't penetrated. Maybe he hadn't said them with enough conviction. Should have said, *Don't go—I don't want you to go.*

What he hoped he'd gotten across in their previous conversations about her leaving the Corps was that she should take some time to think about what she wanted. And was welcome to do it here.

Too late. She'd accepted a job.

In San Diego?

His questions would have to wait until tomorrow.

For the boy's sake he'd been hoping she'd find something around here. Ryder had taken to ranching like a true Henry.

The beginning had been rough. Ryder'd cried himself to sleep through months of bad dreams. Or Hatch would wake up in the middle of the night to find the boy staring at him. Depending on how tired Hatch was at the time, he'd either get out of bed to take the tot back to his room, or give the boy the nod to crawl into bed with him, and hope that he didn't get a knee to the groin for his troubles.

Now Ryder looked forward to visiting Wyoming and their time together. No more bad dreams.

Hatch made his way inside, letting the screen

door close behind him. He shut and locked the interior door. Most folks around here didn't bother with locks. He'd come from a bigger, more dangerous world. Locked doors gave him a sense of security.

And keeping Ryder safe had been his job.

He rubbed the back of his neck and wondered how often he'd get to see Angela and Ryder with this new civilian job of hers. After grabbing another beer from the fridge, he went into his office and turned on his computer to work on a new accounting program he'd been trying to learn.

What a pain in the ass learning something new was.

He picked up one of his grandfather's ledgers, which had found its way to his desk, and opened it to a random page. Every bull, cow, calf and steer accounted for by hand, and it had probably taken the old man less time than if the geezer had used a computer.

Hatch got up to put the ledger back on the shelf and found himself reaching for one of Ryder's recordable storybooks. They hadn't read this one together in a long time, but he still remembered Ryder crawling into his lap with the book. Hatch didn't really know if it was a single memory or an accumulation of memories over time.

But he remembered how he felt.

He'd pushed that button over and over again while they listened to her voice for hours. He never got tired of it. As much as Ryder loved hearing his mother's voice, somehow the kid had gotten across that he wanted Hatch to stop pushing the button and just read to him.

Over the years and hundreds of times they'd read together, Hatch had gotten to the point where he'd memorized each of those storybooks.

Ryder didn't need reading to anymore, and Hatch hadn't realized how much he missed that until now. He put the book away and returned to his desk, wondering if Angela ever thought about having another child.

Instead of settling into learning the new accounting program, Hatch clicked over to indulge in his other guilty pleasure. And wouldn't the guys give him crap if he tweeted it wasn't cyber porn.

"Hi," she said from a tent somewhere in Afghanistan. "I was thinking about what you said. About how much you miss reading a good book because you don't have the time." She paused to lick her lips. Which always got the same involuntary reaction from him. "I thought maybe we could try an experiment. I bought you this book

and the companion book on tape, unabridged."
She held them up for him to see. A military
thriller, Dale Brown's latest at the time.

He'd had to pause the message here that first
time or two because that worthless horseshoe ring
he'd given her during their wedding ceremony
was clearly visible on her left ring finger.

She never wore it when she came around. But
every time they were on Skype he looked for it.
And it was always there.

"Anyway," she continued, "I made you this
tape to summarize each chapter for you. If you
lose your place, you can come back to me to help
you find it."

Closing down the computer, he sat staring at
the blank screen. Their long-distance relationship had evolved over the years into a comfortable one. Online or over the phone, they shared a
connection stronger than just being on the same
cell phone plan to save money.

But he had to wonder where that was going
when she hadn't even clued him in to the news
that she'd become a civilian. Hatch rubbed the
bridge of his nose.

He was always overthinking their relationship.
Especially whenever she stayed under his roof.
Which, thank goodness, wasn't that often. Be-

ROGENNA BREWER 193

cause tonight the ache in his groin had little to do
with a kid crawling all over him.

When he'd found her out on the porch and
she'd raised her arms to dry her hair, the gap between her pajama pants and top revealed a flat,
toned belly. And nothing on under that tank. Just
cold, hard, wet nipples straining against fabric left
damp by her hair.

Twenty-seven looked mighty fine to him.

The images of their one night together liked to
taunt him, but mostly they came back as feelings.
Like the one of being buried so deep he wanted to
die.

If she had been more experienced at the time,
he might have proposed something more mutu-
ally satisfying. Something that didn't leave him
sitting alone in the semidarkness of a quiet house.

Like sharing a bed.

But adding those marital privileges would only
complicate their already complicated situation.

The only thing stopping him now was that he
cared too much to make it about sex.

Accounting program all but forgotten, Hatch
rolled out the blueprints he'd left leaning against
his desk. At one time Hatch's dad had commis-
sioned an architect, paid a pretty penny for these
drawings.

When he thought he'd stick around. Build a new house and leave Hatch's mother to hers. Hatch had been thinking about that house more and more this last year and the fresh start it represented.

The foundation had been laid years ago. Now it was time to build on it.

CHAPTER ELEVEN

ANGELA CLOSED HER LAPTOP and reached over to turn off the bedside lamp. After talking to Jake, she'd tried to settle in with a good thriller. But she felt on edge. Which had nothing to do with the tragedy of this particular room.

She liked to believe Hatch's mother and sister were smiling down on him for all the improvements he'd made to the house and ranch. And that in having done so, he found his past no longer haunted him.

Hatch and Ryder had made this room over in soft creamy colors for her years ago.

A nice neutral palette.

To which she'd added nothing. Not one personal touch. She hadn't even unpacked her seabag tonight. And she wouldn't. It would be ready to go when she was.

Unfortunately, she'd just learned online that it wouldn't be this Saturday or even next Saturday. It took twenty days from filing to get a divorce in Wyoming. It took sixty days to establish residency in order to even file for divorce.

Coiling and uncoiling a strand of hair around her finger, she stared at the blank wall across from the bed. To file for divorce would take her eighty days of staying put.

Hatch had to be the one to file.

Getting him to agree to that should be easy enough, right? Except, that was where her uneasy feeling was coming from.

She threw back the covers, got out of bed and went to sit on the windowsill, where she listened to the mooing of the cows wandering close to the fence, and the deeper bawl of the restless bull.

She couldn't track the approaching storm from this side of the house, but the air was heavy with it and smelled of rain.

Closing her eyes, she listened to the rumble outside.

She'd managed to spit out the news about her job, but she'd yet to spell out the repercussions of it. Plus, she still had to let Hatch know the time had come for their divorce. And now instead of her filing, she had to ask him to do so.

Don't go.

She turned his words over in her mind again. Had he simply wanted her to stay and talk? Which she should have done. Or was he suggesting she put off her plans in favor of letting Ryder stay through the Fourth of July?

For an instant, when she'd looked into his eye with that current shooting up her arm, she'd thought maybe those words held a deeper meaning.

As in, stay.

She knew Hatch didn't want her to take the job. And he probably thought the job was in California, even Denver. Not London, England.

BlackWatch had its headquarters in L.A., with satellite offices and operatives around the globe. But they were opening a new overseas division headquartered in London. And Jake anticipated them being there at least a year in order to get the business off the ground.

What would Hatch have to say about that?

They'd had this odd friendship for so long now that he felt entitled to advise her in every major decision of her life. Because she'd given him that authority until now.

What if he said don't go, and she went, anyway, taking Ryder with her? Would that be an end to their uneasy friendship?

How would that affect his relationship with her son?

And what was that relationship exactly? Would a clean break be best? Jake had talked about adopting Ryder once they were married.

And he did say he liked that she wasn't a ticking biological clock, like most of the women he'd dated. That it made him want a family.

So if she'd like to go off the Pill...

At some point she'd be adding to her family. And although she wouldn't have said it six years ago, she could see Hatch wanting to start a family of his own.

He might need a couple years to figure it out, but she imagined he'd find a big old void somewhere around the middle of his chest once he realized he didn't have Ryder six months out of every year.

And he'd get drunk one night, trying to fill it. While some down-on-her-luck stripper, whose name he wouldn't even remember in the morning, would wind up pregnant.

He'd marry her because it was the right thing to do. Wouldn't even ask if the kid was his. And they'd live happily ever after.

So really, what was the sense in dragging this out?

The bull wasn't the only one restless tonight. Hatch had been moving around downstairs for over an hour now. Angela didn't know how late he planned to stay up. And even though he had to get up early, she should just go down there and tell him.

But before she could put her foot to the floor, she heard him mount the stairs. Heavy steps meant he was exhausted. Because although a big man, he could move with the stealth of his Navy SEAL training when he wanted to.

Her heartbeat picked up, the way it always did when he was near. He'd turn right toward his room. But she found herself holding her breath until that moment passed and his door opened, then closed with a quiet click.

There was a time after that first deployment when she'd listened with her ear to her door for him moving around in his room across the hall, and thought about going to him. What had stopped her then was not what stopped her now.

While she'd never regretted their one night together, her days of creeping across the hall were over. That kind of intimacy made their marriage vulnerable to the expectations of what a real marriage should be. Hers, at least.

Like forsaking all others.

His relationships with other women were none of her business.

But she couldn't quite explain the disappoint-
ment she felt that he'd never once taken a left to
knock on her door.

And she was no longer free to knock on his.
She was engaged. She could only hope that would
feel a lot more real after she divorced her husband.

THE FOLLOWING DAY, Hatch returned to the house
after morning chores to find a tight little ass in
gray yoga pants with her head in his refrigerator.

She reached in, revealing thong panties and a
tramp stamp across her lower back. Whoa, that
was new.

"'Morning," he said, hanging his hat on a peg
by the door. With her earbuds on, she didn't hear
him.

She pulled back and closed the door with a
yogurt cup in her hand. Yogurt was something
you wouldn't normally find in his refrigerator,
except he'd had his housekeeper stock up with
Angela's favorite foods.

She yanked an earbud out when she saw him
standing there. He caught a snippet of Beyoncé
and "Run the World (Girls)" before she turned off
her iPod. "'Morning."

"'Morning," he repeated.

"Is that the hat I bought you online?"

He glanced back at his cowboy hat by the door. "You mean the one I get razzed about because it came from California."

"There are cowboys in California." She peeled back the yogurt lid and licked it before tossing it into the trash.

"Yeah, but they're all transplants."

Settling back against the cupboard, she rolled her eyes and set about eating her breakfast.

His gaze dropped to where the pink sports bra barely covered her breasts, let alone her midriff. The open sweat jacket, also gray, had afforded only a glimpse of skin from behind. He liked this view better.

For a woman to get that much muscle definition she either had to be taking 'roids or doing about two hundred sit-ups a day. Her hair was pulled back and he noticed the beads of perspiration on her brow. "How far'd you run?"

"Three miles."

He moved to the fridge, though he wasn't hungry.

For food, anyway. She had a glow about her that he attributed to running, but it left him with an uneasy feeling. "Going easy on yourself today, huh?"

"I did just drive how many miles yesterday?"

"Is that why you slept in?" he asked, looking around in the fridge for nothing in particular.

She reached over and swatted his arm, and he closed the door of the Subzero empty-handed. "You could have woken me up," she said. "Did you get Ryder off to school okay?"

"We have our routines." Driving him up to the main road to wait for the school bus every Monday through Friday was one of them.

Hatch could have allowed Ryder to ride his bike up to the mailbox and chain it there for the ride home, the way Hatch had done as a kid. But their short commutes in the morning and occasionally the afternoon gave them time each weekday to catch up.

Most afternoons, weather permitting, he'd hike or jog that mile up the road and they'd have a nice long walk back to talk about their days.

"Though I will say, with you here and this being the last week of school and all, he did not want to go today."

"Can I ride with you this afternoon to pick him up?" She threw her empty yogurt cup into the recycle bin. "Or will that mess up your routine?"

He reached around her for a glass in the cabinet above her head and she slid along the counter to give him room at the sink. He ran tap water into the glass despite the cold water in the fridge. "I can never tell if you're teasing me."

He hadn't meant to say that.

Did she really think he was so regimented?

Okay, so maybe he was a little habitual about his schedule. But he wasn't that bad. Was he?

"I'm not teasing. Not about that." She held his gaze before dropping hers.

Whatever teasing had been going on dropped with it. This was as good a time as any to pick up where they'd left off last night. "Have you made a decision about the job?"

"Yes," she said.

He nodded, accepting her answer for what it was. And ignoring the pang he felt somewhere near his chest. "And the county fair?"

He'd promised Ryder he'd ask again. He hadn't mentioned the job to the boy because breaking that news was his mother's business. But maybe the start date was negotiable.

"About staying through the Fourth of July, you mean?" She tugged on her ponytail—which she often did when she was anxious about something. "Actually, yes," she said, letting her hair fall to her shoulder. "I did some online research last night."

She took a deep breath. "Now is probably as good a time as any to give you that divorce I've always promised. And that will allow us just enough time to get through it."

"Sounds good." He drained the glass he'd been holding for no good reason.

"If it's all right with you, I'd like us to tell Ryder together. When we pick him up this afternoon?" She'd tried to make her words sound upbeat, and wound up sounding forced.

"Sure," he replied.

"Okay."

"I've got a full day of work ahead of me."

"Is there anything I can do? You know I'm used to working with men. And used to following orders."

And not much good at being idle.

"Can't think of a thing." He set his glass on the counter.

"Mend fences, herd cattle? Dress deer?"

She'd meant to be funny. He knew she didn't know the first thing about his cattle operation. But he was always saying he wanted to show her the ropes. Why not today?

He should have picked up on the part about the deer.

Of course he remembered that. He remembered everything that was important to him.

She watched him all the way out the door, expecting him to…what? From the moment they'd said, "I do," a divorce was what he'd wanted. What they'd both wanted.

So why'd she feel so crappy right now?

"Aren't you even going to ask?"

He turned around. "Darlin', I don't have to ask. I'm only surprised it took this long for someone to find you." He grabbed his hat from next to the door.

"Meet you back here at three?"

He tipped his hat on the way out.

Wow, seriously. No reaction from him at all.

No *I'm so happy for you.* Or *Tell me about this guy you just met. Where'd you meet him? Where's the ring? You sure that rock's not cubic zirconium?*

Or *He's not good enough for you!*

I thought I warned you away from Special Ops guys.

Where was the relief she should be feeling? Instead, she felt as drained as the glass left sitting on the counter. She picked it up and loaded it into the dishwasher.

It wasn't like Hatch not to pick up after himself. Because of his mother, he never left anything sitting around.

CHAPTER TWELVE

"LOOKS LIKE BIG RED just kicked you in the balls." His foreman entered the stables, letting a stream of sunlight in with him.

Hatch stood off to the side, backed up against a stall. The pain in his gut had him doubled over, and he was finding it hard to breathe.

"Go away," he said without conviction.

Smitty closed in on him. "What'd you do this time?"

"How long does it take to get a divorce in Wyoming?"

"That bad?" he asked. "Twenty days from the day you file."

Hatch took a couple more deep breaths and forced himself upright. Pressing his back against the stall, he slid halfway down into a crouch. The pain had subsided, but not the panic.

He rarely had these kinds of panic attacks anymore. The last one he remembered was before he'd even met her, shortly after his return from Iraq.

But this morning, one minute he was walking out toward the equipment barn to check on a tractor, and the next he was doubled over in the stables.

Sensing his distress, the three mares left in their stalls were pawing at the ground and snorting.

"Seems to me," Smitty said, "when a man feels physical pain at the thought of divorcing his wife, he might want to think twice about it."

"Don't be ridiculous. I've been praying for the day I'd get her off my hands."

He just hadn't realized how the thought of her with another man would affect him. He should have recognized that glow on her face. The only time he'd seen it was when she'd been lying naked across his chest, staring down at him with those incredibly innocent eyes.

What an idiot he was.

The tattoo. The thong.

They screamed sex.

"You do realize you're the chick in this relationship, don't you? You have to be the one to tell her how you feel."

Hatch glowered at his foreman, then dropped

his head into his locked hands. "I don't know how I feel. Part of me is relieved."

Or should be relieved, since he'd always believed this was exactly what he wanted. They'd stay together until she found someone else.

Well, she'd found someone.

"You've got twenty days to figure it out," Smitty said, turning a feed bucket over to sit down on, so that they were at eye level. "Of course, maybe you put off filing until you're ready."

"She'll just file."

"She can't."

Hatch lifted his head.

"She's not a legal resident of the state. And she has to have been for at least sixty days before she can file for a divorce. She hasn't lived here ninety consecutive days in six years. Ran into that problem with my second wife. No good run-around that she was took off to Montana with—"

"Smitty, I could kiss you right now."

The older man scowled. "If'n you're that horny, you might want to start by moving your wife into your bedroom."

That wasn't an option.

But filing for a divorce ninety days from now was better than filing today. Especially when it meant she had no choice but to stick around.

"You ready?" Hatch stood in the doorway.

Angela was sitting at his desk in the den when he showed up at three o'clock on the dot. She'd found his jumbled notes for a new accounting program. "I hope you don't mind," she said. "I thought maybe I'd take a look and see how I could help—"

"Knock yourself out." His expression remained impassive. But at least he hadn't objected to her helping.

The contrast between his stoic acceptance of their divorce and the pictures he'd surrounded himself with was mind-blowing.

They were smiling in every one of those photos.

The picture of her and Ryder dressed like pirates. The Halloween following her first deployment, her son had insisted they each wear a black eye patch. She hadn't been exactly sure how that would go over with Hatch, but it had sort of become their thing.

The following year he'd had Ryder for Halloween and they'd dressed like monsters. Ryder as a mummy and Hatch as Frankenstein.

Both with fake bloody eyeballs popping out.

"These are good memories, aren't they?" Angela murmured.

"You're not going soft on me now, are you?"

She just might. Her favorite memory had nothing to do with Halloween. It came from another year, in which he'd kept Ryder to the end of school and then driven him to San Diego.

Hatch hadn't stayed long.

Two weeks. And with one of his SEAL buddies.

During the day he'd gone to the base and harassed the BUD/S in training while hanging out with the SEAL instructors. He'd been offered an instructor position that would have brought him out of retirement and back into the field he loved.

She'd kind of hoped for Ryder's sake that Hatch would take the job. Yet he'd returned to Wyoming and she didn't hear any more about it. But she had her suspicions.

She knew city driving freaked him out.

In fact, she'd done most of the driving during those two weeks. She thought that maybe one too many close calls on busy streets had made him eager to return to a less populated area.

That and the fact the ranch had started to take off, so he'd had to choose one over the other. But she'd never forget that was the summer he'd taught them to surf.

In the picture the three of them wore wetsuits

and were monkey-piled on top of a surfboard, Hatch on the bottom, her in the middle and Ryder on top.

She hadn't realized how long she'd been staring at that photo until Hatch cleared his throat. "You ready?"

She picked up her purse and followed him out to the truck. To reach the mailbox required only a few minutes. Hatch checked for mail as if that was part of his routine. Routines were very important to him. She wondered if he'd ever strayed from his rituals.

Although she hadn't spent much time at the ranch over the past six years, the prospect of not spending any time at all here in the near future once again saddened her.

They should be talking about how they would answer Ryder's question about their divorce. Instead, they waited in silence a few minutes more before the big yellow school bus rolled to a stop and Ryder got out.

He waved to the driver and his friends still on board the bus, before climbing in the backseat of the truck.

Angela shifted around in her seat. "How was your day?"

He shrugged. "You know. Last week. We didn't

do much. Cleaned chalkboard erasers. Cleaned out lockers, that sort of stuff."

She doubted that was all they'd done, but she let his remark go. Hatch turned the truck around and she realized the ride back was so short they might not have the time they needed.

Since they hadn't discussed how they were going to proceed, she took the lead. "Say, you know how I promised we'd spend more time together soon?"

Ryder nodded and she continued, "And you know Hatch married me so I could join the Marine Corps," she prompted. "Now that I'm getting out we won't need to stay married."

"Okay, cool."

"Cool." She'd managed to get through her explanation without using the *D* word. And Ryder seemed fine with the news.

Slanting a glance toward Hatch, she wondered if he thought the explanation too simplistic for an nine-year-old. She'd expected more of a reaction from Ryder, just as she'd expected more of a reaction from Hatch this morning.

"One more thing," she said to Ryder as they pulled into the yard. "We'll be staying through the week of the Fourth."

"Yes!" Her son pumped his fist.

"But I don't want any more outbursts like the other day, or we'll leave right then and there. Understood?"

When had she started sounding like a mom?

Ryder hopped out of the truck. "Will we be moving again when we get back to San Diego?" he asked with the long-suffering sigh of a military brat who'd moved too many times to count in his young life.

What Hatch had provided for her son was stability. But she'd be able to provide that from now on.

"We are." She left things at that as he scrambled into the house, eager to dump his backpack. One more day and for a whole summer he wouldn't have to worry about lugging it around.

"You didn't say much." She'd followed Hatch toward the equipment barn.

"Wasn't much for me to say." He didn't really have a destination in mind. He was just trying to put some distance between them. It wasn't working.

"You must have something to say."

They'd reached the SteelMaster, a big aluminum building with a sliding door on each end and four garage doors on each side. Here he housed his equipment.

"Plenty." He slid one of the end doors wide without another word.

He'd been thinking about their marriage—or rather, pending divorce—all day. About his expectations six years ago compared with today. And to be honest, not much had changed.

"Would you prefer I stay at Maddie's?"

"I would, but he wouldn't." Hatch nodded toward the house.

Hatch still wanted her, and he was going to lie his ass off about it. From that day to this, he'd been waiting for one thing: her to grow up.

He could have had her years ago.

If he'd been willing to clip her wings.

"Are we going to spend the whole month fighting? Or just not talking?"

"Probably."

The barn was one big open concrete bay. He passed the stall with the tractor he'd been working on, and headed for the far corner.

"I'm getting married in six weeks."

Six weeks? "How long have you known this guy? And how come I haven't heard anything about him until now?"

She crossed her arms. "I met him on the flight home."

"I suppose you love him." Hatch tried to keep the contempt from his voice. Most people didn't know what love was. He sure as hell didn't. "And he loves you."

Even when it was staring him in the face.

"I wouldn't be standing here asking you for a divorce otherwise."

If you love something, set it free. If it comes back to you, it's yours. If it comes back demanding a divorce, you're screwed.

"I'll file," he agreed. He didn't need sixty days or even sixty minutes to figure out what he wanted. Or to realize that it might be too late. "On one condition."

"You want Grandma Shirley's pink Cadillac," she said, guessing at what lay beneath the tarp.

"No," he said, removing the car cover. He just wanted to show her he'd been taking care of the old Caddy. The way he'd been taking care of Ryder.

And maybe she'd see beyond that to why.

Plus, he did have one really big demand that would probably piss her off. So he wanted to be in a place where she wouldn't start throwing things. "I want shared custody."

"You'd better be talking about the Cadillac and not my son."

CHAPTER THIRTEEN

As far as bombs went, he'd dropped a pretty big
one. She'd had no idea he felt that strong an at-
tachment to her son. She knew how Ryder felt
about Hatch. But Hatch played his cards pretty
close to his chest. Angela had stood there in the
aftershock and accused him of trying to use Ryder
to manipulate her.

Words she wished she could take back.

To be fair, Hatch hadn't known they'd be moving to England. When he found out, he dropped
all demands. And settled for so little she wanted
to cry at the unfairness of it. Two weeks a year at
the ranch.

As if his wanting less meant he loved Ryder
more, she felt self-centered and selfish. Friday
rolled around, and despite their agreement, he
still hadn't filed for a divorce. He wanted those
two weeks in writing.

Which meant he didn't trust her to do the right
thing.

Angela sat at his desk, going through the books as she switched them over to the new accounting program—

"Clay said to set these on his desk."

Angela looked up to find a brunette with big brown eyes staring at her. The young woman handed her the mail.

"Hi, I'm Emily. The housekeeper."

Housekeeper? She was kidding, right?

Angela hadn't actually said that, but she'd wanted to. Emily was young and pretty. And only a bachelor would hire girlfriend material to pick up after him.

Maybe she was the girlfriend, and housekeeper was the term they were using for Angela's benefit. Not that they needed to bother hiding their relationship. "Angela. Adams," she added unnecessarily.

"I know, Clay's wife."

"Soon to be ex-wife."

"I know."

"Oh." Angela didn't know what to say to that. Apparently Emily knew everything.

"I'll unload the groceries and get to work."

Smiling politely, Angela nodded and set the mail aside to get back to work herself, when the bill on top of the mail pile caught her attention.

She and Hatch had their cell phones on the same plan to save them both some money.

Her name was on the statement with his, so she didn't think anything about opening the envelope. Had the man never heard of electronic billing?

She could set him up in a matter of minutes. And while she was at it, she'd separate their accounts.

"Wait a second." Her name was on the bill.

Her name was also on a couple pieces of junk mail that had been delivered. And the statements for their joint bank account. The one she deposited into for child care.

Seeing all those statements started the wheels spinning. She opened drawers until she came across a year's worth of cell phone bills in both their names.

She didn't have to establish residency. Residency had already been established for her.

With a little online research, she found the military loophole she needed to file for divorce as a resident of Wyoming.

It was all she could do not to grab her keys and go.

But he could trust her to do the right thing. So she'd wait it out. So they could talk. After everything she'd said to him, she didn't want him thinking she was trying to pull a fast one on him.

The sound of the vacuum upstairs had her glancing at the clock. It was five after three. *Five after three?*

She did grab her keys and go then.

Hatch's truck was still parked outside. It wasn't like him to vary his routine. She spotted him walking toward her from across the compound.

"Did you forget the time?" She rushed past him.

"Don't think so." He checked his PalmPilot. "No," he said with conviction.

"What about Ryder? Shouldn't we be leaving to meet his bus?" This was the last day of school.

"He's spending the night with Alex."

And nobody had bothered to tell her that. "Since when?"

"Every Friday night since he's been here."

She should have known. And she should have realized something was up when Emily had delivered the mail. Hatch normally collected it when he picked up Ryder from the bus.

Emily stepped out onto the front porch. When Jason—auto parts Jason—stepped up to meet her, Angela did a double take.

The two kissed, a little too passionately for

having an audience, and then strolled hand in hand toward Jason's apple-green Dodge Charger.

"'Night, Clay. 'Night, Angela," they said in unison.

"'Night, Em, Jason." Hatch nodded. "Recognize your old beau?"

"He was only interested in my pink Cadillac." Nice to know he could still tease her about that. "Jason works for you now?"

"Couple days a week. Helps keep the equipment running."

"Emily, too."

"Same deal, couple days a week."

The place cleared out fast on a Friday night. The hired help had plans to paint the town red. Even Smitty pulled out a few minutes later, leaving Angela and Hatch alone.

"And what is it you do on Friday nights?" she dared ask.

"Same as everybody else. You want to come?"

She hestitated because her first instinct had been to say yes. And she'd had to remind herself she was engaged. "No, thank you. I don't think so."

RYDER SAT IN FRONT OF THE TV at his friend Alex Stewart's house, playing Mario Kart. Same as he did every Friday night. Will came home from work with a pizza. And Mia let them eat it in the living room as long as they were careful not to spill their pop on the carpet.

"Hatch and my mom are getting a divorce." He put his whole body into moving Mario around the track.

"Bummer," Alex said.

"Yeah," Ryder agreed. "We're moving again, too. I wish we could stay here."

"Yeah. Me, too." Alex found a break in the action long enough to manage a bite of pizza and glance back over his shoulder at his mom and stepdad. And his annoying little bother, Anthony, who was four. He had a sister, Sophia, who was seven, but she was at a slumber party tonight. "My mom's going to have another baby."

"Yeah." Alex called Will "Dad," even though he was his stepdad. "I wish Hatch was my real dad," Ryder stated.

"He's your stepdad."

"Technically, no," he said, repeating what his mother always said.

"Yeah, he is. He's married to your mom, right?"

"Yeah."

"That's all it takes to make him your stepdad."

"I guess." Ryder watched annoying little Anthony crawl all over his mother's lap, until Will picked him up and carried him off to bed. Mia stood to stretch her back, and Ryder couldn't help but notice the baby in her belly. "Do you think if they had their own kid they'd stay together?"

"Yeah, maybe."

But Ryder's mom and stepdad didn't even sleep in the same bed. Half the time they didn't even sleep on the same continent.

CHAPTER FOURTEEN

"MOJITO," ANGELA SHOUTED above the din. "A real one. Not the kind that comes in a bottle."

"Huh?" their waitress asked for the second time.

"Two beers. And two mojitos. The kind that come in a bottle is fine." Hatch held up two hands, two fingers.

"You just changed my drink order," Angela said, somewhat amused by his need to always take charge. She hadn't planned on going out with him tonight. But when she couldn't get ahold of Jake, her big plans for staying close to the phone for the evening had changed.

"No bartender likes to make those fancy drinks on a busy Friday night." Busy because a local singer by the name of Dusty was back in town for the first time since signing a major record deal.

Hatch had sent her the CD while she was in Afghanistan.

"FYI." She leaned forward and toyed with the

candleholder in front of her. "No date likes to be told what she can and cannot order."

"Are you my date?" he asked with equal amusement.

"No, I'm your soon-to-be-ex-wife. Just thought maybe you could use the dating tip." She stared at the candle flame, recalling those dating tips he'd given her all those years ago. Advice she'd never followed.

He met her halfway across the small round table and lowered his voice. "Where did we go wrong?"

It was so not what she'd expected to hear that she didn't even think about telling him that she planned to file for divorce on Monday. With or without him.

Their waitress saved her from having to answer right away by setting a napkin in front of her. And the truth was she could choose not to answer. Angela sank back in her seat while Hatch settled the bill.

"You didn't do anything wrong, Hatch."

"Something happened between us."

She ignored her drink in favor of peeling off the label on the beer bottle. "A lot of things have happened between us over the years. Most of them good."

"But that one night wasn't?"

"See, you're twisting my words."

"What's the point of all this now?" He'd had six years to ask her that question, and she found it more than a little disconcerting that he chose to ask it now. "Maybe the issue here isn't my sneaking out but your not trying to stop me."

There. She'd said it. He hadn't tried to stop her.

He'd made love to her. He'd stopped her from saying she loved him. And he'd simply let her go.

Admitting that hurt made her feel exposed. And she still didn't see the point of revisiting the past.

"Thank you for being honest."

"That's it? That's all you want from me?"

"I just want you to be happy, Angela."

"Clay?" A redhead closer to his age than hers approached their table. "I thought that was you, darlin'."

The woman completely ignored Angela as Hatch struggled just to recall her name. He should have defaulted to admitting he couldn't remember, and allowed the woman to fill in the blanks. Not in this case, however.

Angela had a sneaking suspicion she didn't want to find out how he knew this woman.

"Excuse me," he said to the other woman. "I'm here with my wife."

"May I have this dance?" He held out his hand to Angela.

She placed her hand in his and he led her out onto the crowded dance floor. The band was playing a cover of Rascal Flatts' "Bless the Broken Road."

"Your wife?" she said, looping her arms around his neck.

"I didn't know what else to call you."

He was teasing her again. She thought she'd become better at compartmentalizing.

Consider it a dance and it's just a dance.

But when she felt those tingles of anticipation where his fingers trailed her spine, oh, boy, was she in trouble.

In the military the ability to compartmentalize was a necessary part of survival. She couldn't walk around with her head in the clouds or she'd likely trip herself up. She had to stay grounded in reality. Focused.

Concentrate on the task at hand.

Watch where she stepped and be aware of her surroundings at all times.

But she couldn't do that here, not with him. Not for another twenty minutes.

Let alone twenty days.

Not when the instant she let her guard down all those old feelings came rushing in. No wonder one or the other of them picked a fight after two or three days.

She had a new name for fight or flight.

All her senses were screaming. Put out or get out. Fast.

"So how do you know the redhead?"

He seemed to gauge his words. "What if I said I honestly couldn't remember?"

"That makes it ten times worse."

"I honestly can't remember."

"Have you slept with her?"

He stopped dancing. "Not once in six years have you asked me that question." He sounded more than just a little irritated. "You don't get to be engaged to another man and ask me that."

THE DRIVE HOME WAS a silent one. The tension in the cab of the truck was so thick he couldn't have cut it with a hacksaw. She shouldn't ask him personal questions if she really didn't want to know the answer.

And if she didn't like the answer, tough.

"Do you really want know?"

He'd startled her with the question, he could

ROGENNA BREWER 229

tell. She cast a sharp glance in his direction. She'd understood immediately what he was talking about. She'd been thinking about it.

Had he slept with the redhead?

She wanted to know, all right. She wanted to know because she wanted an excuse, any excuse, to pick a whopper of a fight. And he was ready for it. If that was what it took to get it all out in the open, so be it. Either they'd get beyond this or they wouldn't. He glanced at her reflection in the windshield. The cab was dark and he could barely make out her features in the reflected glow of the dashboard lights. "Come on, let's play our own version of the newlywed game. How well do we really know each other?"

"Yes, I want to know," she snapped. "As if I don't know the answer already."

"She's someone I knew from high school. I didn't recognize her at first because she's lost a lot of weight," he said, letting that sink in. "I didn't sleep with her then. And I sure as hell haven't slept with her since."

"Okay, so you haven't slept with her."

He turned down the ranch road.

"Now ask me how many women I've slept with since we first met." As she studied his face he could only look at her through the reflection.

"But don't ask it unless you're prepared to hear the answer."

He pulled up in front of the ranch house and parked. "You want me to believe," she said, "that you haven't slept with another woman since the day we met."

"Call me old-fashioned. It was also the day we married."

"It wasn't that kind of marriage."

"No, it wasn't," he agreed. "I thought I'd be divorced in six months, so why not wait? And that wasn't exactly a period in my life when I was looking for companionship. Six months later I had Ryder for a year and a steep learning curve."

"But after that—"

"Was right after we slept together. The truth is, six years later I don't know why the hell we're still married."

He stared at her. She stared at her hands in her lap.

"What if I'm not ready for this to end?" he asked.

She looked at him then. It didn't matter that there was a console in the way. He reached across that divide and kissed her. Her lips parted in surprise as he tested his limits. Tasted that minty mojito.

"No." She pushed against his chest. "You had six years to kiss me, Hatch. You can't kiss me now. Not like that."

THE CLERK EYEBALLED Angela above her reading glasses. "Take a number, please."

Angela wondered if she should point out that there was nobody else here. But the woman already knew that and just wanted to exert her authority.

So Angela took a number and waited while the ten numbers ahead of hers were called. She wouldn't be surprised to find the woman had ripped the numbers off herself just to play games with people. Angela was in no mood for games.

She was here to file for divorce. She touched her fingers to her lips. The sooner the better. Hatch had kissed her last night like he'd meant it. But maybe the only thing he'd meant by it was that he didn't like to lose. Because he'd certainly never made a move before the threat of losing both her and Ryder.

Ryder had left with Hatch for the feed store earlier in the morning. She was going to find it hard spending time with her son while avoiding her husband if the two of them were always together.

Finally her number was called and stepped forward. "I want to file for divorce."

"You're Clay's wife?"

"Yes."

"Then I'm afraid you can't," the woman said with a smug smile.

"I have proof of residency." Angela dug a handful of bills and statements out of her purse and showed them to the clerk.

"Clay filed this morning." The woman threw that out like a bad punch line. "That makes you the defendant. Will you be contesting these divorce proceedings, Mrs. Miner?" she inquired.

"It's Angela Adams," she said. "And, no. No, I won't be contesting this divorce."

"Why don't you save the sheriff a trip out to the ranch and pick up your summons next door. I'm surprised Clay chose irreconcilable differences. He should have chosen by reason of insanity. You are crazy to let that man go!"

Angela left the clerk's office and headed over to the sheriff's department in the same building. As luck would have it her summons was still in their office and they were happy to let her sign for it.

Stepping outside, she heard her name—well, Mom—and turned to see Ryder waving from the passenger seat of Hatch's truck. Like the man driving it, the truck had a lot more mileage on it these days. They all did. He checked his rearview mirror and slowed to a stop in the middle of the street as she walked up to her son's open window.

"Hi," she said, including them both.

That side was Hatch's blind side, so he had to turn in his seat to be able to see her. "We're heading back now," he said.

He glanced at the legal document in her hand, recognizing it for what it was, and met her gaze head-on. His lips were pinched—with regret?— and seeing it made her own smile feel forced.

The countdown to the end of their marriage had begun.

They'd waited this long. Three weeks wouldn't kill them.

And hopefully, they wouldn't kill each other.

"ALEX FINDS THIS BORING," Ryder whispered later that evening as the three of them were lying in wait in one of Hatch's deer blinds. "But I know you'll like it."

"I'm certain I will," Angela whispered back.

Hatch cast her a glance over Ryder's head as if to say they were doing too much talking and not enough waiting. That her nine-year-old even knew this was called a kill plot was a bit disconcerting.

"It's just a name, Mom," he said. "You don't hunt fawns or their mothers."

But mama deer had a spot nearby and stopped for a quick bite on the way to the feeding grounds. The fawns were old enough now to follow her.

And sure enough, after sixty minutes of waiting, twenty minutes in total silence, they saw the doe and her spotted twins. Hatch passed the binoculars to Ryder, who took a peek and passed them along to Angela.

A short while later the deer moved on from the grassy knoll, but the three humans continued to stare in awed silence. Broken at last by her son's awkward assertion.

"Hatch, if you wanted to make a baby with my mom, that would be all right with me."

"That's good to know," Hatch said, as though they were talking about the weather. He pushed himself to his feet and offered her a hand up. She hesitated and he dropped his hand to his side.

"Don't get too far ahead," she said to her son as he bolted toward the ranch house. "How in the world would he come up with something like that?" she asked as he took off.

"Who knows." Hatch shrugged.

"He's lonely for a little brother or sister, I guess." She nibbled on her thumbnail. "Do you figure he understands where babies come from?"

"Trust me, he understands. It goes on all around him. And we talk."

"Yeah, but I'll have to have The Talk with him."

"If you want me to…"

She must have blinked.

"What—you don't trust me?"

She crossed her arms. "I just don't know what you'd say…"

"Well, I'd make sure he's got his facts straight. And I'd answer any questions."

"What would you tell him about love?"

"It's not a necessary component of sex. Or baby making."

"Yes, but what would you tell him?" That he didn't have an immediate answer was telling. "You don't believe in love?"

"I don't believe in a lot of things."

When it came to words and emotions, Hatch was as *tight-lipped* as his name implied. She'd figured it out her first time aboard a ship. The area around a hatch was called the lip and when it closed it formed a watertight seal—a seal that held provided watertight *intergrity*—in Navy terms. Which meant he'd earned his nickname for being a vault of integrity. The keeper of secrets.

A closed hatch.

She just wished he'd open up to her sometimes.

"HATCH?" HE AWOKE TO his murmured name. "Hatch, wake up." Opening his eyes, he noted with his monovision the glowing face of the alarm clock and Ryder's worried one for the third time that week.

"What is it?" He propped himself up.

"Mom's having a bad dream."

Same as last night. And the night before.

Hatch rolled over to go back to sleep. "Your mother's a big girl. She can handle her own nightmares. Go back to bed," he ordered.

Ryder tried to shake him.

Hatch rolled onto his back and gave the kid his stink eye, which was what they called his single-eyed stare. "Ryder," he warned.

"Please, Hatch."

The kid looked as scared as Hatch had ever seen him. Like the time ol' Blue got hit out on the highway and they had to rush him to the vet. He glanced at Blue now and the dog whined.

"I heard her crying."

Rubbing away the last vestiges of sleep at two o'clock in the morning, Hatch reached for his eye patch on the nightstand and couldn't find it.

Screw it.

He kicked back the covers and got out of bed. He'd learned a long time ago there was no sleeping in the buff with a kid around. Hatch didn't bother putting anything on over his shorts for the quick trip across the hall.

Her door was cracked open, as if Ryder had already peeked inside. Hatch heard her thrashing around in bed before he reached it. Her mostly incoherent mutterings were speckled with colorful language and the words *No, don't.* And *Stop.*

"Go back to bed, Ryder. I've got this." He nudged the boy toward his own room. To his surprise, Ryder didn't argue. Blue followed Ryder back to bed. The heeler had had his own pillow in the boy's room from the time he was a pup. Charlie on the other hand, as a highly disciplined bomb-sniffing dog, slept kenneled in the kitchen at night. For now, anyway.

"Ange," Hatch said sharply.

She paused momentarily. But didn't wake up.

He pulled the rocking chair closer to her bedside and tried to recall if you were or weren't supposed to wake someone from a nightmare. Or was that sleepwalking?

And what was all that nonsense about waking up from a falling dream before you hit the ground?

He'd fallen plenty of times in dreams and in life, but couldn't ever remember that feeling of hitting ground until he'd met her. Hatch liked to think he'd landed on his feet. Only he wasn't quite so sure he'd landed yet.

He leaned forward in the rocker and went with a different tactic. "Angel." He took her hand in his. "I'm right here. It's okay now."

His murmured reassurance seemed to calm her.

Assuming these were post-traumatic dreams, he wondered at the trauma she'd been left to deal with. In a way he was lucky. He couldn't recollect anything surrounding or following the trauma of losing his eye. Nothing that kept him tossing and turning at night, anyway.

He sat in the chair, watching her sleep, until he felt himself drifting off.

ANGELA AWOKE TO the rooster's crow. Lifting her head from her pillow, she found Hatch staring at her.

Her gaze dropped to their linked hands.

"You were having a bad dream," he said, disengaging.

"Did you sit in that chair all night?" she asked.

"Something like that." He stretched the kinks in his neck. "Sorry about the other night."

She leaned back against the headboard.

They'd barely spoken a word since. The dreams had surfaced that night. Bits and pieces of something buried so deep she'd almost forgotten it was there until her past collided with her present to remind her.

"I saw a woman stoned to death." And she'd been absolutely powerless to stop it. "We weren't allowed to intervene. Though we tried. And she managed to escape. We found her the next day."

Angela remembered straining against the gunny, who'd held her back as their CO argued with the town's leaders for leniency. Angela had shouted her own protests, to no avail.

Hatch stared down at her for a moment. "Move over."

She quirked an eyebrow.

"Don't look at me like that."

She scooted back toward the center of the bed and he sat beside her. She didn't protest.

She simply wanted him to hold her. "Hatch,

have you been with anyone else since we've been married?"

"No, ma'am. I have not."

She felt those first tears escape.

"Shh," he said. "If you want to make a fashion statement we'll get you that scarlet letter. But nobody's throwing stones. Least of all me."

"It wasn't supposed to be this complicated," she said, turning into his side.

"Angela," he said, rubbing her back, "it was always going to be this complicated."

CHAPTER FIFTEEN

Fourth of July County Fair

THE SWEETWATER COUNTY FAIR in Rock Springs, Wyoming, was a seven-day event that opened on a Sunday and ran through Saturday. The main gate and the midway opened at 4:00 p.m. every day, with concerts and fireworks well into the night.

Angela knew the county fair was a big deal to Ryder. She just hadn't realized how big a deal it was to Hatch. But somehow he convinced her they had to leave the house at 6:00 a.m. because the livestock gates opened at 7:00 a.m.

The Fourth of July fell midweek, but Hatch had been driving up to Rock Springs every morning since Sunday. He'd leave at dawn, pulling an empty trailer, and return by noon, hauling more livestock. She and Ryder would spend their mornings with Char and Blue, getting the cattle dog ready for his trials, and when Hatch got back the three of them would sit down to lunch together.

Then they'd tag along with Hatch for the rest of the day. Following orders came second nature to her and Ryder knew when to stay out of the way. Rather than shooing them off like the pests they were, Hatch always found something for them to do.

Angela had to admit their routine felt comfortable. A sense of calm came over her unlike anything she'd known before. She was no longer a young single mom struggling to get through each day.

And no longer free-falling from thirty thousand feet.

She'd landed.

The Marine Corps had a saying: pain is temporary, pride is forever. Against all odds she'd turned her life around. Not without sacrifice.

But for more days like this one, she'd do it all over again.

"I love you. You know that, don't you?" She put an arm around Ryder as they left the area where Blue was kenneled. Trials began a half hour from now, at 10:00 a.m. And Ryder had drawn a number in the middle of the roster of thirty competitors. "Good luck out there today."

"Mom," Ryder said, eyeballing the competition. "You're embarrassing me."

"That's what mothers are for." Hatch ruffled her son's hair as Ryder walked off with the other kids in his division for their precompetition handler meeting.

They'd bought Char along to keep Blue company, and they'd been checking on the dogs and exercising them, as they'd continue to do throughout the day. Angela was more worried about how Ryder was going to hold up.

They joined Maddie in the bleachers and waited for the cattle dog trials to begin. Earlier, they'd strolled through the livestock pens and sat through an auction in which the prize-winning bull had gone for an astronomical price. Angela noticed Hatch didn't bid on any of those overpriced bulls. Most of his business was conducted while talking to other ranchers.

So she wasn't surprised or offended when he volunteered to get them water and didn't come back right away. She and Maddie chatted over the program of events and mapped out the rest of their day. If Ryder made it to the finals they'd be back here at 1:00 p.m. If not, well, they'd still be back to watch.

By the time Ryder was on deck the metal bleachers had worn a groove in Angela's butt and she shifted uncomfortably. The young girl ahead of him couldn't catch a break. Her dog had responded to every command by doing the opposite.

Nervous laughter escaped from the audience when she had a hard time getting the animal to leave the arena. Finally the dog exited ahead of her, and the crowd acknowledged her efforts with polite applause.

"Here you go." Handing out bottles of water, Hatch stepped over the bench from behind.

"Good timing." She took a sip and set the bottle aside.

"Handler Ryder Adams," the announcer was saying, "with Blue." Three Angus calves were released from the opposite end into the ring.

Ryder gave a barely audible command. "Head 'em out." At the same time he raised his arm as Hatch had taught him, and the heeler took off at a dead run toward the cattle.

"It's okay," Hatch said, as Angela squeezed his thigh. He covered her hand with his. "There are no points for commands, only execution."

Maddie leaned in. "An outrun is worth twenty points."

Twenty out of one hundred.

Go, Blue. The dog circled behind the three calves, herding them toward the chute. The calf on the left threatened to break away, and Blue moved from back hooves to front.

Back and forth. Side to side.

There were points for a weave pattern.

And circling the post to one side.

Blue kept the three calves together and forced them into the open-ended chute. He stopped the lead calf from coming out the other end, then backed off and lay down to stop the clock.

Ryder called the dog back, letting the three calves reenter the ring. "Blue, walk up."

He walked up to the calves for a standoff.

"Watch."

The dog held them in place and then lay down in front of them.

"Head 'em out."

Blue drove the cattle back to their pen and nudged the gate closed behind them. Hatch was on his feet clapping as Blue ran back to lie at Ryder's feet.

Angela bounced up and joined the applause. They'd seen only three other dogs ahead of Blue manage that trick. "That's a perfect score."

Hatch smiled at her. "That puts them in the finals."

"Ryder and Blue walk away with a score of 100," the announcer said. Though they all knew it

got harder from here on out. Sorting cattle. Loading trailers.

Ryder shot them a huge grin over his shoulder.

Hatch cupped his hands and shouted loud
enough to Ryder to hear over the clapping, "Atta
boy!"

Angela could hear the pride in his voice. Could
see it in his face. And felt it in his heartbeat as he
drew her into a sidelong hug that lasted long after
the applause died.

RYDER AND BLUE WENT ON to win third place overall in the junior division of the cattle dog trials.
"Next year," he said, happily skipping along the
midway, "I want to teach Blue some more tricks
and enter him in the freestyle division, too. And
Char. That would be okay, Mom, wouldn't it? So
she won't get bored now that she's retired from
the service."

Listening to Ryder's plans, Hatch watched Angela's smile become tight. Clearly, she didn't want
to ruin the moment by reminding her son they
might not be here for dog trials next year. And
Ryder, happy to have his mother home, didn't
seem to grasp all the implications of her leaving
the service.

And the pending divorce.

Hatch didn't want to dwell on that, either. Life was too short for anything except living in the moment. Even if that moment was at the county fair with seventy thousand other fair-goers in the middle of the hottest July on record. There was nowhere he'd rather be right now.

He looped his arm around Angela's neck, startling her into glancing at him. The truth was he'd surprised himself since he'd implemented that long-ago look-but-don't-touch policy when it came to her.

Ryder was holding his mother's free hand, and Hatch drew Maddie into the fold by placing his other arm around her. When had anything in his life ever felt this right?

"What do you say we let your mother show off some of her skills?" They were strolling along and stopping at whatever games interested them. He steered them toward the shooting gallery and slapped down a twenty. "We're going to want that bear, right there."

The stuffed bear in question being bigger than Ryder. The carny offered an indulgent smile. A one-eyed shooter wasn't much of a threat. Hatch wanted nothing better than to prove him wrong, but he went for something subtler than showing off his own marksmanship.

He handed Angela the laser rifle and negotiated a practice shot. The target appeared deceptively simple: a wheel of yellow ducks continually moving counter-clockwise. He'd be surprised if the entire bull's-eye was light sensitive, as implied by those targets. But a decent shooter could compensate.

Angela took aim, fired and missed her first shot.

"Aim to the right of your target." He backed up that suggestion by realigning her body to the right. She'd have to hit all twenty in a row, at a dollar a shot, to win the big prize.

Ping. The first duck went down with a cacophony of distracting sound effects. And on down the line, in rapid-fire succession, she targeted light beams on twenty ducks in a row.

The carny handed over the big bear with a reluctant grin, knowing he'd been had by a couple of pros.

TOTING THE STUFFED BEAR on her hip like an overgrown child, Angela got out the sunscreen while they stood in line for the Ferris wheel, and slathered some on Ryder. "Your neck's getting red."

"Mom." He squirmed away in embarrassment.

"What about mine?" Hatch asked.

She reached up behind him and wiped the remaining sunscreen on her hand across his heated skin. "Your neck is always red."

"A little redneck humor there?"

"If the boot fits…"

"Then I hate to tell you this, but hand over that sunscreen."

She squeezed some into his palm so he could rub it on her exposed back. The lotion felt almost cold on her skin, making her shiver. They'd begun the day wearing several layers of clothing, and more than a few trips to the truck later they were all down to as few as possible.

He started with her neck, and then moved to her shoulders around the knot of her racer-back top. The longer he went on the more it felt like a massage. And just when it started to feel really good he stopped.

"Mom, I'm going to go sit with Maddie," Ryder announced.

"What's wrong? Too many corn dogs and snow cones?"

"Nothing's wrong. I just want to sit down."

"Next!" The guy who ran the Ferris wheel was calling them forward as Ryder stepped out of line.

Angela would have followed, but Hatch nudged her toward the ride. "He's fine."

Still, she kept her eyes on Ryder those few moments it took him to get to the bench where Maddie was resting her tired feet. Angela waved before stepping inside the cage. She had a love-hate relationship with Ferris wheels and held on to the bear in the seat between them. She loved the way Ferris wheels looked all lit up at night. Hated the rocking motions as they began to turn and then stopped.

Moved and stopped.

She and Hatch inched their way upward.

She rested her chin on the bear's head. "How'd I let you talk me into this?"

"I seem to recall this was your idea." His smile seemed indulgent. "Afraid of heights?"

She shook her head. "Falling."

THEY SAW IT AT THE SAME time, an unfamiliar car parked outside the house. Ryder had gone home to spend the night with the stewarts and Maddie had taken off with the judge after they'd all met up for the evening concert and fireworks. Hatch suspected their friends and family of trying to set them up. But the truth was he and Angela had a pleasant drive home alone with Char and Blue kenneled in the back of the truck. And he'd anticipated making the most of this moment.

What he hadn't counted on was the intrusion of a stranger.

Hatch got out of the truck and Angela followed.

"Jake?" She got out and walked straight over the driver's side of the other vehicle. The dark-tinted window rolled all the way down. "What are you doing here?

"Thought I'd surprise you."

"Well, you did that."

The other man got out of the car. "Aren't you going to invite me in?" he was asking.

That's when Hatch recognized him. By his voice. And in the way he carried himself. "Jeager?"

Son of a bitch.

She'd gone for an older guy. Jeager had a couple years and a couple gray hairs on Hatch, at least.

He was ex-Special Ops, at that.

"Hatch?"

Theirs was a small community of operatives. At any given time there were only so many Navy SEALs in service.

They'd served around the same time.

And right after he'd gotten out, Hatch had done some contract work for BlackWatch.

Courier work. Cairo, Egypt, mostly.

The father ran the company back then.

"You two know each other?" Angela looked as if she was about to faint. And dammit, Hatch wasn't going to catch her if she fell. But he moved in closer just the same.

"I guess we do at that." Jeager eyed him carefully.

Hatch folded his arms and tucked his hands into his armpits to keep from punching the guy.

Here it was, after midnight, and they were standing out in the middle of the yard. Hatch supposed he should offer to put him up for the night.

In Ryder's room.

But before he could make the gesture, Angela came up with a different solution. "Why don't I take you over the boarding house? You'll be more comfortable there."

ANGELA FOUND THE KEY Maddie kept underneath the flowerpot on the front porch. It wasn't breaking-and-entering if she'd been informed of its existence and invited to use it at any time.

She led the way to the rosebud room, because it was the one room she knew she could find her way to in the dark. Besides Hatch's room. And she wasn't about to let Jake stay there.

"Kind of weird, huh?"

That Hatch had been a contract employee with

BlackWatch at one time? And that they had both been with the Teams. She hadn't realized just how compartmentalized her life had become until her fiancé and husband came face-to-face and realized they knew each other.

"Yeah, kind of," she agreed, keeping her voice to a whisper. She didn't want to wake Maddie. If Maddie was even home yet.

Jake dropped his bag to the floor.

"Missed you." He pulled her to him for a kiss.

Which quickly turned into an I-want-to-show-you-just-how-much-I've-missed-you kiss. Even though it had been only a couple days.

Angela extracted herself. "Not here," she pleaded. "This is his aunt's house. It wouldn't be right."

Respectful was the word she'd been looking for.

But really, it was just too weird.

Especially since Hatch had told her he hadn't slept with anyone else.

"Not here, not at the ranch. I should have driven you to the Red Carper Inn up the road while I had the chance," Jake teased. Or maybe he wasn't teasing.

And maybe he should have.

There was one flaw to her logic in bringing him here. She couldn't just drop him off and have

Maddie wondering about the strange man in her house. And Angela couldn't spend the night with him.

"I'm going to be right across the hall," she said. She didn't have any other choice. And not so much as a toothbrush with her.

They kissed a final good-night kiss.

And she crossed the hall, half expecting Hatch to be completely moved out, now that he'd had his own place for a while. But the room was just as she remembered it.

Which really sucked. Except that she didn't feel all that bad about using his toothbrush or raiding his drawers for something comfortable to sleep in. She was, however, disappointed to find the scrapbook she'd made him all those years ago. Until she opened it and discovered he'd added pages chronicling these past six years.

Then she felt like a snoop, looking at pictures of her and Ryder. And occasionally, ones with him in them.

She stopped digging and opted for a plain white T-shirt. And a pair of boxer shorts that hung somewhere around her hips. His clothes smelled like clean laundry, but the pillow when she crawled in bed smelled like Hatch. That fresh clean Irish Spring scent she'd once had a hard time identifying.

Rolling onto her back, she turned her head away from the memories. And then rolled right back.

What made her think she could spend a night in this room and not think about *that* night? And really, how dare he try and turn it all around, to make it about her leaving.

A person had a right to her feelings even if those feelings weren't reciprocated. She should have just said it, and to hell with him.

I love you.

I'm sorry you don't like the word. Or is it that you don't trust the word? Or maybe it's that you don't trust the feelings?

But you made me feel that way. So what are you going to do about it, huh? Huh?

But it was too late.

Those feelings were no longer relevant. She was no longer that young, or that naive. She'd changed her fairy tale so that it at least had some basis in reality.

Jake was her reality. And he was amazing.

So why was she in a bedroom across the hall from her fiancé, trying to push her husband from her mind? The AC kicked in and the temperature dropped dramatically. The room felt like a meat locker.

She got up to adjust the thermostat.

Seventy-two degrees wasn't all that cold, but she boosted it up a couple notches. Shivering, she tiptoed back to bed and buried herself deeper beneath the covers.

The rattle and hum of the air conditioner threatened to keep her awake. It was the middle of summer, for crying out loud. Most people slept with air-conditioning. She wondered how many of them were sleeping alone.

CHAPTER SIXTEEN

HATCH HAD JUST RETURNED from taking the boys to Grainger's so Ryder could show off his third place ribbon when Angela and Jeager showed up in the rental car. Hatch locked on to Angela across the hood of his truck. She could barely meet his eye.

"Who's that?" Ryder asked.

"Friend of your mom's." It wasn't Hatch's place to say.

This is Mommy's friend Hatch.

And that was Mom's fiancé, JJ.

"Oh," the boy said, quickly losing interest even as she was motioning him over. "Do you think we could take Mom to see the fawns again tonight?"

He roughed the boy's hair. "Why don't you go see what your mom wants? Maybe she'd got plans for this evening."

He didn't have to ask where she'd spent last night. He knew she'd taken her *fiancé* to Maddie's. But like an idiot, Hatch had waited up half the night for her return.

Just to talk.

For some reason he'd been under the mistaken impression that she was coming back to the ranch, to sleep in her own room, in her own bed—after she dropped Jeager off.

"Can Alex and I play paintball?" Ryder persisted.

"*After* you check in with your mom."

Hatch wanted to be civilized about all this, even though he was feeling anything but. So he turned his attention to work and headed to the pens. When Ryder and Alex slipped past him, heading in the direction of the deer blind, it was the first time Ryder had ever deliberately disobeyed him.

Hatch was about to call the boy back when he decided to join the rebellion. *Screw it.* If the kid wasn't ready to meet the new man in his mom's life, then he wasn't ready.

"Anything I can do to help?" Jeager asked a while later. They were castrating the bull calves today, with Blue picking them out of the herd, running them through the chute. It took three men, doing it the good old-fashioned way.

Two to hold the calf, one to clamp it.

Hatch already had three men on it.

Besides, he couldn't see Jeager stepping in

cow pies with those three-thousand-dollar Italian leather loafers on his feet.

"Sure," Smitty said. "Why don't you hold the hind legs."

"Oh, okay," Jeager said. "Sure."

"Put on some rubber boots first," Hatch suggested. He nodded toward the barn so the man knew which direction to take.

"You really want that city slicker helping?" Stew asked, wrestling the next bull calf down the chute into submission.

"I really want to see him kicked in the nuts," Smitty said, holding on to the other side.

Hatch put the clamps down on the testicles and squeezed. He released the banded calf to be eartagged farther down the chute.

Jeager returned with rubber boots and work gloves, taking up Smitty's position on Hatch's left. The foreman had seriously underestimated the ex-SEAL. He made it through the hour without being kicked.

And without allowing Hatch to be kicked. Of course, that was a matter of opinion.

"I didn't realize you grew up on a farm," Jeager said.

"Does this look like a farm to you?"

"Is there something you want to say to me, Hatch?"

There was plenty he wanted to say, but he held his tongue. "I think we're communicating just fine."

Clamp and squeeze.

RYDER AND ALEX WERE hiding out in the deer blind, playing Mario Cart on their handheld Nintendo DS game systems. They'd been there over an hour and still hadn't seen the fawns.

"I think my mom has a new boyfriend."

"Yeah, that's what it looks like." Alex munched on a bag of chips. "Can we go play paintball now? This is boring."

"Yeah, sure."

Maybe that guy had gone back to wherever it was he'd come from. He probably didn't want to meet a kid, anyway. So the boys got up and started walking back to the house.

Yesterday had been better than any birthday present, Ryder decided. They'd been like a real family. He and Blue had taken home a ribbon and that made everyone happy. Then, after Maddie said something about falling in love on a Ferris wheel, he'd had the brilliant idea of letting his parents ride alone so they could fall in love.

He'd thought it worked, too.

They got all gooey-eyed, or as gooey-eyed as Hatch could get, just before the fireworks when Rascal Flatts sang "Bless the Broken Road"—as if that song meant something to them. And they hadn't spent the day trying hard not to touch each other, as they usually did.

Mom even talked about wanting to go back the rest of the week for the concerts. Everything was perfect. Until they got home and that guy came along and ruined it. Now that sick-to-his-stomach feeling Ryder had from eating too much junk wouldn't go away. Only he hadn't eaten much of anything all day.

"There you are." His mom and Char came up to them as they were leaving the pine grove. She'd probably brought Char along to sniff them out. "You boys can't wander off like that without permission."

"I asked Hatch if we could go to the deer blind." Ryder felt his cheeks grow hot and hoped his mom couldn't tell he was lying. It wasn't really a lie, because he *had* asked.

She frowned at him as if she saw right through him. He petted Char, hoping the black Lab couldn't sniff out a lie, because Hatch said a dog had to be able to trust its trainer. That's when

Ryder noticed the big shiny ring on his mom's finger where she sometimes wore that cool horseshoe nail.

He scowled back at her.

"There's someone I want you to meet." She steered him toward the corral, where Hatch was talking to that guy.

"Come on, Alex," Will said. "We've got to get home in time for lunch."

"What about paintball?" Alex asked, as he was led away by his dad.

"Bye, Alex." Their days for this summer, at least, were numbered. Ryder tried not to let it bother him that they didn't even get the chance to play with his new paintball guns. "Maybe you could spend the night on Friday."

He looked at his mom, who didn't like him extending invitations without permission. He was getting himself into all kinds of trouble today. "We might not be here Friday," she said in a low, quiet tone.

Last night Mom had wanted to hear more concerts at the county fair. Today she talked as if she didn't know what she wanted, or was on someone else's timetable—like when she was a Marine. And had to do what they told her to do.

Hatch didn't have anybody telling him what to

do. And when Ryder grew up nobody was going to tell him what to do, either. He was just a kid, but he knew exactly what he wanted, and it wasn't meeting this guy.

"Jake, this is my son." She beamed at them both. "Ryder, Jake is my fiancé. He's asked me to marry him."

Some fancy smancy word for the guy with his arm around his mom, about to ruin his life. It meant his mom wasn't just getting a divorce from Hatch, she was going to marry someone else. But what if Ryder didn't want another stepdad? He kept stealing glances at Hatch, expecting him to say something, but he was just standing there with his Grim Ripper face from Guitar Hero. Which was better than his Death face from Dante's Inferno video game.

"Nobody asked my permission." Ryder ground out the words.

"Ryder," his mother scolded.

She seemed more embarrassed than upset.

"No, he's right," Jake said. "We're just sort of springing this on him." Tall and dark like Hatch, the man crouched down to Ryder's level. Only Ryder wasn't a little kid any more, and Hatch had quit crouching down to talk to him a long time ago. "I hope you and I can become good friends,"

Jake was saying. "And I'd really like your permission to marry your mother. You'll like it in London. I have a nice flat there—"

London? Who said anything about moving to London?

"*No,* you can't marry my mom!"

"Ryder!" This time she snapped at him.

Only Jake seemed amused by Ryder's show of temper. He pushed back up to his full height. "Okay, so now we both know where we stand."

"No, it's not okay. Ryder, apologize this instant."

"I don't want to move to London!" London was about as far away from Hatch and Wyoming as they could get. "I want to stay here and live with Hatch."

"You can't stay here—"

"Then I want to go live with my *real* dad!"

ANGELA FELT AS IF she'd been slapped in the face.

Three months after a night of underage drinking, her son's *real* dad hadn't even remembered her name. He'd accused her of lying, of sleeping around. He didn't want to hear the baby was his. Even though she knew the baby couldn't be anyone else's.

She'd made her choice that day. And he'd made his.

Which was why the boy's birth certificate read "Father unknown."

Anything she said right now would only escalate the situation. Even Hatch didn't have his usual calming affect on her son. Ryder stormed off toward the stable.

And both men stood there looking at her.

She turned on Hatch. "I suppose you think there was a better way for me to handle this?" She propped her hands on her hips, daring him to challenge her parenting.

Because that's what he'd done these past six years. He'd challenged her. Made her a better parent. But there was no such thing as a perfect parent.

She'd had three choices. Break the news over the phone. Tell Ryder when she first arrived, while his temper was still hot. Or wait until things cooled down. Well, excuse her for picking the least confrontational choice.

And for her bad timing.

"I didn't say anything," Hatch said. "Are you sure you want to start this fight?"

She'd planned on telling Ryder. She hadn't planned on Jake showing up, impatient for her divorce proceedings to be over with. Which only showed how much he cared.

If he still cared after seeing what a rotten mother she was. So rotten her own son picked his stepdad over her.

She took a step toward the stables. "Give the boy some room," Hatch suggested.

ANGELA STORMED OFF in the opposite direction from her son. Hatch and J.J. were left staring at each other. "I'd better go check on her," Jake said, moving toward the house.

Hatch wandered into the stable. Even before his vision adjusted to the dim light, he heard the boy crying. Ryder was up against Daisy's stall with his head bowed, shooing the mare away while she gently nudged him.

Blue was sitting at the boy's feet.

"You don't really want to go live with your dad."

"Yes, I do," Ryder stubbornly insisted. "You're my dad. I want to live with you." He launched himself forward and wrapped him in a fierce hug. "I love you, Hatch."

Hatch hugged the boy back. "I love you, too." He brushed his red head, so like his mother's.

And so unlike Hatch's own. "You do know I'm not your biological dad?"

He felt compelled to ask that. Hatch assumed Ryder knew—the kid had been told—but he didn't really know what was going on in the boy's head.

Ryder nodded. Good to know Hatch hadn't screwed up the birds and the bees that much. "When you're older, and not just trying to hurt your mom, I'll help you find your father—if that's what you want."

Angela would cringe to hear him say that. But the boy had a right to know. And coming from a male perspective, if Ryder were his son, *he'd* want to know. She'd just have to get over it.

She and Hatch hadn't always agreed on how to raise the boy, but they'd always compromised in his best interest.

"What about your mom?" Hatch asked. "You love her. You'd miss her if you came to live with me."

"She could live with us." Ahh, so that's where he was going with all this.

"She doesn't want to live here," Hatch acknowledged around the lump in his throat. "But I promise you, I will always be in your life. And you can come visit me whenever your mom will let you. We want her to be happy, don't we?"

Ryder swiped at his tears and nodded.

"Well, he makes her happy. *You* make her happy," Hatch added, tweaking the boy's nose. "And I have a feeling the two of you are going to get along fine." He lifted Ryder's chin so the kid had to look up at him. "Give him a chance and in a few years you'll have everything you ever wanted."

Because what the boy really wanted was a family.

Parents who loved him and a little brother or sister, maybe more than one sibling. Yeah, it was all going to work out for the kid.

And with that realization came the knowledge that all that had been within Hatch's grasp, and he'd chosen to let the merry-go-round wind down, and to not reach for that brass ring.

And look what that was going to cost him when he was forced to let go....

He glanced up to find Angela standing just inside the door. Ryder ran to his mother and wrapped him in her arms.

Hatch didn't know how long she'd been standing there, but judging from the appreciation in her watery, moss-green eyes, it had been a while.

"I hate to interrupt." Jake cleared his throat. "Don't you two have a hearing at the courthouse this afternoon?"

SIX YEARS HAD GONE BY in the blink of an eye. And the past twenty days even faster. Angela tore off a number and sat back down between Ryder and Jake, waiting for number forty-five to be called. Hatch sat a few chair away. And Maddie hurried in at the last minute, looking frazzled.

After an interminable wait Angela's number was finally called.

"Oh, honey, you don't need a number," Carla said. "You could have just checked in at the desk. You're on the judge's docket." She lowered her voice to a whisper. "Next time you'll know."

Carla led them into a courtroom and had them take a seat in the back bench, and then walked their paperwork up to Judge Booker T. Shaw. The judge took his time going over it.

It struck Angela as funny that they'd brought more witnesses to their divorce proceedings than to their wedding. She wanted to share the observation with Hatch, and glanced across the aisle. But he remained focused, staring straight ahead, and she was on his blind side and couldn't catch his attention.

The courtroom was a lot less intimate and a lot more intimidating than the judge's chambers. Judge Shaw called them forward. "Clay, Angela," he said, acknowledging them from the bench. "Well, you lasted a lot longer than you antici- pated. Clay, you filed your complaint as irrecon- cilable differences. Angela, you're not contesting. We have no children from this union."

Angela glanced back to where Ryder sat qui- etly, and relatively calmly. She didn't know why he'd insisted on coming, and there'd been no one to leave him with, last minute, when Maddie had insisted on coming, too.

"And no division of property or assets," the judge continued, with no inflection or comment. "You've had twenty days, as mandated by this state, to think it over. Have either of you changed your mind?"

He motioned for everyone in the back row to sit down. "We don't do that here, folks." Angela turned just as everyone was taking their seat again. The Stewarts and Carla joined Maddie there. Poor Jake didn't know whether to sit or stand at this point.

Ryder remained standing in the middle of the aisle. "Could I just state my objection, anyway?"

"The court will indulge the defendant's son."

"I just wanted to say, I'm sure Jake is a pretty cool guy and all, but I'd like to see my parents stay married." Ryder moved forward like a nine-year-old trial lawyer arguing his first case.

"I mean, they managed to stay married this long while living apart and raising me to be a decent kid. Imagine how totally awesome I'll turn out if they stay together. Oh," he added as an afterthought, "Hatch plans his whole day around Skype, and Mom won't pick up the phone if she thinks she's being an imposition."

Hatch rubbed the back of his neck.

Not knowing what to say, Angela hesitated. But something had to be said. And everyone was looking at her.

"You're already an awesome kid. I'm sorry, son, if this day isn't turning out as you'd hoped."

Ryder lowered his voice. "I wasn't the only one looking forward to having you home." He'd said just enough to leave her dazed and confused as he headed back to Maddie.

"Shall we continue?" the judge asked, and then did so without anyone answering. "You've had an extra twenty minutes to think things over. Have either of you changed your mind?"

"No, Your Honor." Hatch spoke into the silence.

Crushing any false hope she may have had. "No, Your Honor," she mimicked.

"Divorce granted."

As soon as the gavel fell, ending their six-year marriage, Hatch couldn't sign the decree fast enough.

And there it was—the reason they weren't staying together. While she'd been standing here thinking he might love her enough, or at least love Ryder enough, to try and make a marriage between them work, he'd been thinking *get me the hell out of here.*

Irreconcilable differences.

Angela picked up the pen he'd just put down.

He stunned her with a kiss to the forehead. "It's been an honor and a privilege," he said, for her ears only.

He turned to leave before she'd even signed. He stopped to shake hands with Jake. And then bent to say something to Ryder, rumpling her son's hair on his way out the door.

Everyone was looking at her as if she was supposed to do something instead of just stare after him. Sign...she was supposed to sign. It wasn't legal until she signed.

She'd be crazy to run after a man who didn't love her. Except everything in her heart was telling her he *did* love her. He'd never spoken those words, but he'd shown her in so many ways. In the way he'd taken care of her and her son.

Coming here today, because he thought she wanted him to. Because she'd thought she wanted him to. Was it possible he loved her that much? Enough to stand aside and let her marry another man? She looked at Jake. A man she knew loved her.

But did she love him enough?

Even Jake was nodding toward the door.

And then she did something that shocked and upset everyone.

She signed the divorce papers.

"I'm going to need a copy." Because she loved him that much.

HE'D HAD TO GET THE HELL out of there.

Hatch couldn't stay in the house, either. At least not until she was gone. So he'd taken a bedroll, a bottle of Jack and the new house plans up to his deer blind. The rifle was a bad idea, so he unloaded it into the no trespassing sign before he could get good and drunk.

He planned to celebrate his newly divorced status by getting wasted and burning those cursed blueprints.

No, he'd celebrate his freedom.

That was the only way to look at it. For six years Angela and her kid had taken over his life, and now he was finally free to do as he pleased. Even if that meant spending the next six years in a deer blind.

He was about to uncork the bottle—figuratively, of course, since the damn thing had a screw-on cap—when he caught a glimpse of her hybrid along the ranch road.

"Oh, now what the hell is she doing?"

He sighted down the barrel. She'd pulled off to the side of the drive and was standing in the middle of it with her arms in the air, a piece of paper in one hand.

Only she wasn't circling, or looking off in the wrong direction, because now she knew where to find him.

And then she was making her way toward him, and his heart started to pound. He thought about meeting her halfway, but the truth was, even though he hadn't touched a drop of liquor, he didn't know if his legs would carry him.

So he waited. And waited…

"Hi," she said, handing him the piece of paper. "And you just couldn't wait to bring me a copy of our divorce decree?" He glanced at it and then folded it up to fit in his pocket. "It isn't notarized."

"I was in a hurry." She lowered herself to the ground.

"You're going to want a notarized copy."

When she got married again. He couldn't think why he'd need a copy.

They were quiet for a long time. He didn't want to ask her why she was there. He just figured he'd wait her out and let her tell him.

"What's this?" she asked, unrolling the blueprints.

"A house." He shifted position, bringing one knee to his chest. "I used to think of it as my father's folly. He thought building my mother a new house would change everything. Only he never got around to building it."

Like father, like son.

"That says 'Ryder's room.'" She pointed to the space. "So were you thinking of building this house?"

Hatch stared off into the distance, admitting that would be saying too much. "I was thinking about it."

Let her make of it what she would.

She stopped him from rolling the plans up. "I don't see my room."

"You'll always be welcome in my house, Angela."

He didn't like being regulated to the friendship zone. But the truth was he liked her kid. Correction, he *loved* Ryder. Hatch had said as much today, so he might as well admit it to himself. That boy of hers had swept in six years ago and stolen his love with two candy hearts.

And Hatch had always been helpless to deny Angela anything.

He didn't know if that made him a pushover or a fool.

But there was a reason she didn't see her name on the blueprints. She wasn't reading them correctly.

"I want a room," she demanded.

He pointed at random to a guest room near the master suite. "There."

She studied it for a minute. "I think I'd like that one for the baby's room."

"You're pregnant!" He didn't know why that should surprise him. It sure as hell explained a lot. But he shouldn't have let it color his voice.

"Why would you jump to that conclusion?" She appeared just as shocked. "Out of everything I just said, you heard I'm pregnant?"

She was angry. And he didn't know why. He

had to tread carefully here. Wasn't that what she'd just said?

She shifted in their confined space, brushing against him. Stirring up the air around him with her fragrance. "I suppose you would have stayed married to me knowing I was carrying another man's child?"

"Yes," he admitted, and there was no hesitation or question.

She sucked in a breath. "Hatch, I'm not pregnant."

God, he was glad to hear it. "Then why are you marrying him? You've only known him—"

"I'm not marrying him. That's what I've been trying to tell you. I want to sleep *here*." She pointed to the master suite. "And I want our baby to sleep here." She pointed to the guest bedroom.

"Why didn't you just say so?"

"I thought I did."

What was he missing? "I thought we just got a divorce?"

"We did." She looked down at her hands. The engagement ring was gone. In it's place was the horseshoe nail he'd given her all those years ago. "I wanted you to have the freedom to say no."

"Angela, I'm a big boy. I always had that freedom."

"Are you going to start calling me pet names again?"

"I might," he admitted.

"Well, in that case—" she grabbed him by the shirt collar and put her lips up close to his "—marry me."

It was all he could do to resist. He extracted himself and stood. "No."

"No?" She bobbed to her feet.

"We don't need to get married again."

"You're right," she said with forced cheerfulness. "It's just a piece of paper." She wrapped her arms around his neck. "I love you."

He allowed himself to savor those words on her lips. Hatch didn't want to kiss her again, because he wouldn't want to stop. "It was never just a piece of paper. It was six years of our lives. And I want it back."

"Don't we deserve a fresh start? We didn't exactly have the most conventional of marriages."

"What we need is to catch the judge before he decides he's going fishing. Or home for the night. Because I doubt we'll talk Carla into conveniently losing our paperwork. Convential or not, I love you. And I've loved every minute of being married to you."

The didn't have to talk the judge into anything.

He was waiting for them. Along with their family and friends.

And their son.

The judge ripped up their divorce decree. But just to be on the safe side, they had him marry them all over again. This time with the promises of love, honor and cherish.

And that all-important kiss at the end.

EPILOGUE

ANGELA SLIPPED UP BEHIND her husband to wrap her arms around him. "You don't need to be on guard night after night." She'd found him standing over their daughter's crib, watching her sleep. Chloe had just turned one. Maybe now he'd get a good night's sleep.

"Come back to bed." Angela did her best to entice him. "Tomorrow's a big day."

A few short hours later they were on the road to Denver with the kids in the backseat. Hatch had pulled over in Cheyenne to let her drive.

He'd kept his promise to Ryder and found his biological father. Much to Angela's chagrin.

It was probably one of their biggest fights to date, until Hatch admitted to an ulterior motive: he wanted to adopt her son. And he wasn't going to let anything or anyone stand in his way.

Until that moment she hadn't known it was possible to love him more.

Angela pulled up outside the attorney's office

where Ryder would be meeting his biological father in person for the first time. She wasn't anxious until she recognized him getting out of his car and cutting across the parking lot.

"Is that him?" Ryder asked, a nervous edge to his voice.

"That's him." He looked like an older version of himself from ten years ago. But Angela was surprised to find she didn't feel the same animosity she once had. They'd worked out all the details of this day through attorneys.

She turned to Hatch, who was eyeballing the guy until he disappeared inside. "What's wrong?" she demanded.

"He's going to take one look at the two of you and realize what he's missing."

"That not going to happen. He has a wife and kids, and limited contact after today." The truth was, he was happy to relinquish all rights in order to get out of paying nine years of back child support.

"I like him already," Hatch said. Angela hoped Ryder didn't recognize the sarcasm.

"You're the one who started this whole ball rolling."

"Was there an I-told-you-so somewhere in there?"

"No, but there was an I-love-you in there somewhere."

Ryder leaned forward in his seat, behind hers. She just didn't want him to get his hopes up too high.

"You okay with all this?" Hatch asked, not for the first time since he'd found her son's father.

"Yeah. I just want to say something before we go in," Ryder said.

"Okay." Angela shifted in her seat. He was so grown-up it often caught her off guard.

"Shoot," Hatch said.

"No matter what happens today," Ryder said, "I found my dad a long time ago. When my mom found you."

* * * * *

HEART & HOME

Heartwarming romances where love can
happen right when you least expect it.

Harlequin®
Super Romance

COMING NEXT MONTH
AVAILABLE MARCH 13, 2012

REQUEST YOUR FREE BOOKS!
2 FREE NOVELS PLUS 2 FREE GIFTS!

Harlequin

Super Romance

Exciting, emotional, unexpected!

YES! Please send me 2 FREE Harlequin® Superromance® novels and my 2 FREE gifts (gifts are worth about $10). After receiving them, if I don't wish to receive any more books, I can return the shipping statement marked "cancel." If I don't cancel, I will receive 6 brand-new novels every month and be billed just $4.69 per book in the U.S. or $5.24 per book in Canada. That's a saving of at least 15% off the cover price! It's quite a bargain! Shipping and handling is just 50¢ per book in the U.S. and 75¢ per book in Canada.* I understand that accepting the 2 free books and gifts places me under no obligation to buy anything. I can always return a shipment and cancel at any time. Even if I never buy another book, the two free books and gifts are mine to keep forever.

135/336 HDN FC6T

Name	(PLEASE PRINT)	
Address		Apt. #
City	State/Prov.	Zip/Postal Code

Signature (if under 18, a parent or guardian must sign)

Mail to the **Reader Service:**
IN U.S.A.: P.O. Box 1867, Buffalo, NY 14240-1867
IN CANADA: P.O. Box 609, Fort Erie, Ontario L2A 5X3

Not valid for current subscribers to Harlequin Superromance books.
**Are you a current subscriber to Harlequin Superromance books
and want to receive the larger-print edition?
Call 1-800-873-8635 or visit www.ReaderService.com.**

* Terms and prices subject to change without notice. Prices do not include applicable taxes. Sales tax applicable in N.Y. Canadian residents will be charged applicable taxes. Offer not valid in Quebec. This offer is limited to one order per household. All orders subject to credit approval. Credit or debit balances in a customer's account(s) may be offset by any other outstanding balance owed by or to the customer. Please allow 4 to 6 weeks for delivery. Offer available while quantities last.

Your Privacy—The Reader Service is committed to protecting your privacy. Our Privacy Policy is available online at www.ReaderService.com or upon request from the Reader Service.

We make a portion of our mailing list available to reputable third parties that offer products we believe may interest you. If you prefer that we not exchange your name with third parties, or if you wish to clarify or modify your communication preferences, please visit us at www.ReaderService.com/consumerchoice or write to us at Reader Service Preference Service, P.O. Box 9062, Buffalo, NY 14269. Include your complete name and address.

HSR11

New York Times *and* USA TODAY *bestselling author*
Maya Banks presents book three in her miniseries
PREGNANCY & PASSION.

TEMPTED BY HER INNOCENT KISS

Available March 2012 from Harlequin Desire!

There came a time in a man's life when he knew he was well and truly caught. Devon Carter stared down at the diamond ring nestled in velvet and acknowledged that this was one such time. He snapped the lid closed and shoved the box into the breast pocket of his suit.

He had two choices. He could marry Ashley Copeland and fulfill his goal of merging his company with Copeland Hotels, thus creating the largest, most exclusive line of resorts in the world, or he could refuse and lose it all.

Put in that light, there wasn't much he could do except pop the question.

The doorman to his Manhattan high-rise apartment hurried to open the door as Devon strode toward the street. He took a deep breath before ducking into his car, and the driver pulled into traffic.

Tonight was the night. All of his careful wooing, the countless dinners, kisses that started brief and casual and became more breathless—all a lead-up to tonight. Tonight his seduction of Ashley Copeland would be complete, and then he'd ask her to marry him.

He shook his head as the absurdity of the situation hit him for the hundredth time. Personally, he thought William Copeland was crazy for forcing his daughter down Devon's throat.

Ashley was a sweet enough girl, but Devon had no desire

to marry anyone.

William had other plans. He'd told Devon that Ashley had no head for the family business. She was too softhearted, too naive. So he'd made Ashley part of the deal. The catch? Ashley wasn't to know of it. Which meant Devon was stuck playing stupid games.

Ashley was supposed to think this was a grand love match. She was a starry-eyed woman who preferred her animal-rescue foundation over board meetings, charts and financials for Copeland Hotels.

If she ever found out the truth, she wouldn't take it well.

And hell, he couldn't blame her.

But no matter the reason for his proposal, before the night was over, she'd have no doubts that she belonged to him.

What will happen when Devon marries Ashley?
Find out in Maya Banks's passionate new novel
TEMPTED BY HER INNOCENT KISS
Available March 2012 from Harlequin Desire!

Love Inspired

When Cat Barker ran away from the juvenile home she was raised in, she left more than an unstable childhood behind. She also left her first love, Jake Stone. Now, years later, Cat needs help, and there's only one person she can turn to—Jake, her daughter's secret father. Cat fears love and marriage but a daunting challenge renews her faith—and teaches them all a lesson about trust.

Lilac Wedding in Dry Creek
by Janet Tronstad

Available March wherever books are sold.

www.LoveInspiredBooks.com